Warwickshire County Council

MOBILE LIBRARY SERVICE

06114		
M/Harvood		B T
Catherine Ward		
Helen Lay		
20 MAR 20		

D0493971

This item is to be returned or renewed before the latest date above. It may be borrowed for a further period if not in demand. **To renew your books:**

- **Phone the 24/7 Renewal Line 01926 499273 or**
- **Visit www.warwickshire.gov.uk/libraries**

Discover • Imagine • Learn • *with libraries*

Warwickshire County Council

Working for Warwickshire

013558679X

MR. WHIPPLE EXPLAINS

Mr. Augustus Whipple spends most of his time reading detective stories and thrillers. And his hobby stands him in good stead when he is faced with crimes in real life, for his fictional experiences enable him to find a solution to two mysterious murders, which comes as a surprise to the police and his next door neighbour, Inspector Gallers of Scotland Yard. And Gallers has particular reason to be grateful for Mr. Whipple's hobby when he finds himself arrested as chief suspect for the second murder . . .

GERALD VERNER

MR. WHIPPLE EXPLAINS

Complete and Unabridged

LINFORD
Leicester

First published in Great Britain

First Linford Edition
published 2014

A catalogue record for this book is available
from the British Library.

ISBN 978–1–4448–1978–6

Published by
F. A. Thorpe (Publishing)
Anstey, Leicestershire

Set by Words & Graphics Ltd.
Anstey, Leicestershire
Printed and bound in Great Britain by
T. J. International Ltd., Padstow, Cornwall

This book is printed on acid-free paper

Dedication: To my friend J. HUNT
who first introduced Mr. Whipple

1

INTRODUCING MR. WHIPPLE

'Dear me,' said Mr. Augustus Whipple, in mild surprise and gratification, 'how extremely kind of the Hislops to be sure!'

He peered short-sightedly through his thick glasses at the sheet of expensive notepaper in his hand and read the sprawling message for the second time:

> *East Gables,*
> *Chittering,*
> *Surrey.*

August 10th, 1936.

Dear Mr. Whipple,
  Would you care to come and spend a week here on Friday next, the fifteenth? We should be delighted to see you, and Robert says he is looking forward to beating you at chess.

We shall be only a very small party and therefore everything will be quite informal.

There is a good train from Waterloo at three-thirty so we shall expect you by that.

Very sincerely yours,
Blanche Hislop.

'Really, how extremely kind,' said Mr. Whipple again, laying down the letter by the side of his plate and wrinkling his nose at the whiff of perfume that came from it. 'How very, very thoughtful!'

A vision of East Gables with its cool lawns and scented gardens nestling amid the tree-clad Surrey hills rose before his eyes, and he nodded appreciatively.

London and its environs lay scorching under a week-old heat wave that showed no signs of abating, and the picture was very pleasant. The carefully tended garden of Mr. Whipple's house at Balham was colourful and neat, but not to be compared with that of Robert Hislop's lovely home. Mr. Whipple gave a little anticipatory sigh of contentment and decided to accept the invitation.

As he finished his frugal breakfast he mentally composed the letter which he intended to write in reply.

He was a small, insignificant little man, with thin hair of a nondescript sandy-grey, which he brushed carefully across his bald head in a vain attempt to hide as much of its nakedness as possible. His eyes were weak and rather red-rimmed, and despite his lack of inches he stooped slightly, a habit that added to his general appearance of peering short-sightedness. He affected a certain trim neatness in his attire, was scrupulously careful to wear the correct clothes for all occasions, and was fussy to the point of being finicky over his linen. His voice was timid and there was a touch of the deferential in his manner, so that it was not difficult to supply Mr. Augustus Whipple with the drapery counter behind which he had spent the greater part of his uneventful life.

He exhaled the very essence of the fairly prosperous retired tradesman, which he was. He looked younger than his sixty-five years, was unmarried, and found life a very pleasant thing indeed.

Apart from his garden he had only two hobbies. One of these was chess, a game at which he excelled, and the other was the reading of sensational literature.

The small room which he called his study and to which he made his way when he had finished his breakfast was lined with bookshelves. Here were literally hundreds of detective and crime novels, interspersed with works on criminology. Mr. Whipple was an avid reader, and spent a considerable sum on his hobby. At the Conservative Club in his district he was wont to discuss with authority the latest sensational case occupying the public's attention at the moment, and his fellow members listened with respect to his theories, for was not Mr. Whipple in the unique position of having for a next door neighbour a Detective Inspector of Scotland Yard?

He spent a lot of time talking to the big man over the intervening fence, and Inspector Gallers would listen politely to what he had to say, and although sometimes he smiled inwardly at the little man's theories and suggestions, he always thanked Mr. Whipple gravely and left him with the feeling that his ideas had been of considerable help in bringing the particular problem under discussion to a successful conclusion.

Mr. Whipple sat down at his neat writing table and carefully penned an acceptance of the Hislops' invitation, and as he folded the letter and placed it in its envelope no premonition came to him to offer a warning of the dark and sinister business in which he was to become involved.

He caught the three-thirty train from Waterloo on the following Friday and arrived at Godalming, the nearest station to Chittering, at a little after half-past five. The Hislops' car was waiting, and Mr. Whipple took his place in the back seat with a feeling of comfort and contentment.

It seemed almost impossible now to believe that Robert Hislop had once owned the little grocery shop next door to his own, but then Hislop had always been a better businessman than he. Comparatively quickly 'Hislop's Provision Stores' had spread. Branches had sprung up all over the country, till finally it had been turned into a limited company, and Robert Hislop had eventually sold out his interests.

But he and the little draper who had been his neighbour had always remained friends. Mr. Whipple had been best man at the wedding when Robert Hislop had married the young and beautiful Blanche Edington. He had been a little concerned at his friend marrying a girl so much younger than himself, for there was a difference of thirty-five years between Hislop and his wife. But his fears were apparently groundless, for after seven years he had heard nothing to justify his misgivings.

The car turned into the chestnut-lined drive and deposited Mr. Whipple at the main entrance to East Gables. Droxford, the butler, came down the steps to take charge of his luggage and to offer a dignified greeting. Mr. Whipple was conducted to his room, and after a wash and an extremely careful brushing of his thin hair, came down to the drawing room to greet his hostess

Blanche Hislop was small and fair. The best description of her is dainty and in comparison to her grey and elderly husband she looked little more than a child.

'I'm so glad you were able to come, Mr. Whipple,' she said. 'I don't suppose you will be interested in tennis, but neither is Robert, so the rest of us will forgive you if you both shut yourselves up and play chess.'

Mr. Whipple murmured something about that being more in his line, and was introduced to the rest of the party.

This consisted of four people besides the Hislops. There was a slim, dark girl, whose name was Carol Linden, a young, good-looking man with very shiny black hair and a rather discontented expression, whom Mrs. Hislop introduced as Geoffrey Ryman. A platinum blonde, very platinum and very blonde, whose name Mr. Whipple failed to catch, and another rather older man called Desmond Beal.

This latter individual interested Mr. Whipple more than any of the others. They were fairly ordinary types, the kind of people he would have expected to find. But Mr. Beal was not. He didn't fit. His dark, unprepossessing face wore a sneer, and his eyes held a peculiar amused yet mirthless expression that went very well with the twist of his thin lips. Not at all the kind of person, Mr. Whipple decided, that he would have expected to find at the Hislops'. He took an immediate dislike to the man, which was unusual, and which he realized with inward surprise. Afterwards he traced the beginning of his uneasiness to his introduction to Desmond Beal.

The others had been on the point of returning to the tennis courts when Mr. Whipple had arrived, and Robert Hislop carried his friend off for a drink and a chat.

It was some months since the two had met, and seated in comfortable chairs in Hislop's airy study they talked over iced whiskies and sodas of the things which two intimate friends who have not seen each other for some time usually find interesting.

Big, burly, and red faced, Mr. Whipple thought his friend carried his sixty-odd years well, but there was something different about him which worried Mr. Whipple because he could not place it. And then suddenly, in the midst of listening to Robert Hislop's account of a bathing pool which he was contemplating having installed, it came to him what this strange something was. The knowledge made him a little uncomfortable. Robert Hislop, all the time he was talking was — listening. The something different that Mr. Whipple had noticed, was an air of watchfulness — of vigilance.

The laughter and voices of the tennis players came floating through the open window, but surely these could not be responsible for that unusual alertness? And yet they were, for at that moment Mrs. Hislop's clear voice called: 'Well done, Geoffrey! Game and set to us.' And for the fraction of a second her husband hesitated in what he was saying, floundered, and then with difficulty picked up the thread of his discourse.

Curious, thought Mr. Whipple; very strange indeed. I wonder what is the matter with Robert?

He was still puzzling over this change in his friend's demeanour when he went slowly up the stairs to dress for dinner. That was an occupation that Mr. Whipple liked to take seriously. He hated to be hurried. He was by nature methodical and neat.

He bathed comfortably in the bathroom attached to his room, leisurely insinuated himself into the boiled shirt which had been laid out in readiness, and was engaged in tying his tie when he heard a harsh voice immediately below his window, and the words that it spoke made him pause.

'I'm not going to be put off any longer,' it said. 'That's final. Either you come across with the money or I spill the beans. I'll give you till midday tomorrow, and not a moment later!'

The voice that had spoken was the

voice of Desmond Beal, and the words were so strange and so like a quotation from one of Mr. Whipple's favourite pieces of literature that he felt himself tingling with excitement. To whom had those words been addressed?

Cautiously he went over to the open window and peered out. The speaker had sounded as though he were immediately below, but when Mr. Whipple looked down there was no sign of anyone. He saw the reason for this very quickly. Close to his window the path twisted and passed through a rose-covered pergola, which concealed from view anyone on the path from anyone above. Beyond the pergola was a thick shrubbery. Mr. Whipple withdrew his head and returned to complete his dressing, his uneasiness increased.

There was something very peculiar going on in the home of his friend. This man, Desmond Beal, who looked as though he would have been more at home in a cheap nightclub than in a country house, was obviously threatening some-one. Was that someone Robert Hislop?

And was that the reason for that peculiar, vigilant watchfulness that Mr. Whipple had surprised?

He was intensely interested, and when he descended to dinner he watched the various members of the house party closely. But it was not from the people he expected that he learned anything strange. Robert Hislop was in his usual spirits. Blanche looked radiant, a red dinner frock that enhanced her fair complexion. The unpleasant Desmond Beal was a little taciturn. It was only the slim, dark girl, who had been introduced to him as Carol Linden who was behaving, outwardly at least in any way strangely. She barely opened her lips throughout the meal, but ate in a sort of sullen silence. She was sitting next to Geoffrey Ryman, and once, when that young man addressed a remark to her, her reply was so sharp and snappy as to be openly rude.

Mr. Whipple, looking round the small party, saw Mrs. Hislop frown. It was only a fleeting contraction of the eyebrows and it was gone in a moment. The platinum blonde, whose Christian name was apparently Dorothy, broke in shrilly with a question to Robert Hislop, and the momentary tenseness which Mr. Whipple had experienced relaxed. But it did not evaporate, it was there all through the rest of the meal. The same watchfulness that he had noticed in Robert Hislop earlier in the evening seemed to have attached itself to everyone in the house. He caught them watching each other with covert glances, and once, when he looked up from his plate after a momentary silence, surprised them watching *him*!

Mr. Whipple felt distinctly uncomfortable. He began to wish he had not accepted this invitation. There was something going on at East Gables which made him uneasy, and the more so since it was nothing tangible. He found a comparison in the peculiar, oppressive tenseness that heralds an approaching thunderstorm.

It was with a feeling of relief that he welcomed Robert Hislop's invitation to join him in a game of chess.

They played three games, two of which

Mr. Whipple won, and the mental concentration necessary to achieve this victory wiped, for the time being, every other thought from his mind.

They returned, however, as he slowly undressed that night, and for a long time he stood at the open window clad in pyjamas and dressing gown, looking out into the soft darkness of the summer night.

It was oppressively hot and not a breath of air stirred the leaves of the trees. He heard the soft crunch of feet on gravel and the faint murmur of angry voices, a man's and a woman's.

'You can say what you like!' The woman's voice rose in her anger. 'It's obvious . . . Only a fool . . . '

The man's voice broke in curtly, but in so low a tone that Mr. Whipple could not catch what he said.

'I'll stand no more of it!' snapped the woman. 'You can choose . . . '

They passed out of hearing and Mr. Whipple withdrew into the shadows of his darkened room and taking off his glasses gently polished the lenses. Who the man was he had no idea but the woman who had spoken was the girl Carol Linden.

There was a saying that 'coming events cast their shadows before them,' and if this were true surely the greatest shadow of all would be more potent than any other? Certainly, in spite of the heat of the night, Mr. Whipple gave an involuntary shiver as he got into bed, for the shadow of death which was creeping over the house had, unknown to him, touched him with its edge.

2

MURDER!

The first night in a strange bed always caused Mr. Whipple a certain amount of discomfort and restlessness, and although he fell asleep quickly enough he wakened while it was still dark, and with a vague feeling of disquiet.

In his own bedroom at Balham there was a light switch immediately above the head of his bed. Subconsciously he reached up his hand for this and was disconcerted and irritated to find that it was not there. It took him a second or two before he discovered the reason for its absence and remembered that he was no longer in his own home but at East Gables.

He lay for a little while staring up into the darkness that surrounded him, and then lowering his eyes he saw the oblong of the window lit up with a blue-white

16

light. After an appreciable interval a low rumble came to him, faint, but unmistakable. Thunder.

Thoroughly awake by now, Mr. Whipple sat up in bed, smoothed his scanty hair, and leaning over to a bedside lamp that stood on a small table on his right, switched it on. He did not like thunderstorms. It was not that he was frightened but they produced an unpleasant sensation in the region of his stomach.

Groping for his glasses he adjusted them on the bridge of his nose and looked at his watch. It was a little after two o'clock. Again the window was momentarily filled by the flicker of the lightning. Mr. Whipple, sitting up in his bed, listened for the accompanying thunder, but it was a very long time coming, and he concluded with relief that the storm was a good way from Chittering. He decided that the best thing he could do was to try and go to sleep again, and removing his glasses he put out the light and slid down into his bed, trying to compose himself for slumber.

But sleep had fled. His brain had begun working and he found himself going over the events of the day.

'Dear me, this will never do,' he murmured to himself, and tried to make his mind a blank. But the more he tried the less blank it became.

After twenty minutes or so of futile endeavour he sat up and put on the light again There was nothing for it, he must wait patiently until sleep came once more of its own accord. In his own home, in preparation for such an emergency, he kept a small shelf of books by his bed, but here there was nothing of the sort. There was not even a newspaper. Mr. Whipple propped himself up against the pillow and stared at the window,

The storm had apparently passed, for there was no sign now of any lightning.

For half an hour he sat vainly hoping that drowsiness would overtake him, but instead of anything of the kind he seemed to grow, if possible, even wider awake than before.

'Really!' he murmured, 'this is preposterous! If only I had something to read . . . '

The thought had scarcely entered his mind when he remembered the rows of bookshelves in Robert Hislop's study and came to a decision. He would go quietly down and get a book from there.

He got out of bed and put on his slippers. Pulling his dressing gown round him, he picked up a box of matches, and opening his door stole forth into the darkness of the corridor.

The house was very quiet, and behind one of the closed doors that he passed he heard a faint irregular snore, and wondered who it was that slept so noisily.

Robert Hislop's study was on the ground floor, a large room that lay next to the big drawing room. Cautiously Mr. Whipple negotiated the staircase and found himself in the hall. Here he received something in the nature of a shock. Looking towards the door of the room he was seeking, he saw that it was ajar and that there was a light inside. He came to a dead stop. Who, besides himself, was up and wakeful at that hour?

Since it was Robert Hislop's study from which the light shone so steadily, the natural answer seemed to be Robert Hislop, but it occurred to Mr. Whipple that it might quite easily be some altogether unauthorised person — perhaps a burglar.

He stood motionless in the dark, his dressing gown wrapped round his small figure, his heart pounding noisily in his chest, not daring to move, his eyes fixed on that bar of light. And in the silence he heard the clink of metal against metal.

If the truth must be told his immediate impulse was to hurry back to the security of his bedroom with as little delay as possible. The picture of a ferocious and desperate burglar rose before his eyes — a man who would probably resent, very strongly, any interference from Mr. Whipple in the successful carrying out of his nefarious plan — and the picture was not pleasant. In the silence and darkness of that house it was distinctly terrifying!

By an effort, however, Mr. Whipple mastered his desire to flee precipitately, for although his courage was not a very strong point his curiosity was, and he experienced an overwhelming wish to find out who it was who was moving about in the early hours of the morning in Robert Hislop's study.

With his heart still fluttering he crept nervously across the intervening expanse of hall. There was no sound now from the room with the light, and holding his breath Mr. Whipple peered in. The door cut off a good portion of the apartment but he was able to get a view of the desk and its occupant, and a sigh of relief escaped him when he saw that it was not the ferocious burglar his imagination had pictured but his host. Robert Hislop was seated at his desk, and judging from the fact that he was fully clothed, had not yet been to bed.

Mr. Whipple was about to make his presence known when he became aware of what his friend was doing, and caught his breath in his surprise.

Hislop was engaged in carefully cleaning a revolver!

As Mr. Whipple watched he laid aside the cloth with which he had been wiping the barrel and picking up a small green box began to fill the chambers with cartridges. It seemed to Mr. Whipple a most strange proceeding. He was not surprised that Hislop kept a revolver in his study; it was quite possible he did this as a precaution. The house was a lonely one and its contents valuable. It was quite permissible to suppose that Hislop might own a revolver in case of burglary, but what was peculiar was that he should be up at half-past two in the morning cleaning it and reloading it.

Mr. Whipple saw him spin the cylinder and place the pistol in one of the drawers of his desk, and then it struck him that his own position might be open to false construction. It was in was in any case exceedingly bad form for him to spy on his host. Perhaps the best thing he could do was to get back to his room and forgo the book of which he had come in search. There was no reason why he should not have made his presence known, but to his mind there was something distasteful in being found prowling about the house at that hour.

If it had been half-past two in the daytime instead of half-past two in the early hours of the morning he would have had no hesitation. Convention was an ingrained part of his nature, and he felt more or less guilty of an indiscretion.

Turning noiselessly, he tiptoed back across the hall and made his way up the staircase. A few moments later he had reached the security of his apartment, and removing his dressing gown, kicked off his slippers and got into bed. And curiously enough, now that he no longer desired to sleep, would have wished rather to have dwelt on the curious spectacle he had witnessed of Robert Hislop cleaning his revolver, he found it impossible to keep awake. His eyelids became suddenly as heavy as lead, and he had barely time to remove his glasses and switch off the light before consciousness left him. And he slept dreamlessly until he was wakened by the maid with his early morning cup of tea.

Breakfast at East Gables, he discovered, was a more or less haphazard meal. Blanche Hislop took hers in bed, and did not put in an appearance until later in the morning. The blonde girl, Dorothy, Mr.

Whipple would have preferred to have done likewise, for she kept up a running fire of inane chatter, putting questions which nobody answered and indeed giving them little time to answer if they had been so inclined. Carol Linden barely acknowledged his 'good morning,' but nibbled at a slice of toast in scowling silence. Only Robert Hislop seemed to be in good spirits, and chatted about the programme for the day with the other men of the party.

His air of vigilance, however, had not deserted him. If anything it was more marked.

Mr. Whipple was puzzled, curious, and uneasy. He was a sensitive little man and he felt that there was something wrong about the atmosphere at East Gables. The same tenseness that he had noticed during dinner was again in evidence.

Robert Hislop carted him off after breakfast to show him round the grounds, knowing how interested he was in gardens. And certainly those at East Gables were worth seeing.

At half-past eleven his host left him

with the excuse that he had some business to attend to, and Mr. Whipple, attracted by the sound of laughing voices, made his way to the tennis courts. Here he discovered the blonde-haired girl and Carol Linden playing a set against Geoffrey Ryman and Desmond Beal. Mr. Whipple knew nothing about tennis, but having nothing else to do he stayed and watched. The two men won, and Beal declined the suggestion of another game. Slipping on his coat, he lit a cigarette and strolled back towards the house.

The blonde girl, Dorothy, caught sight of Mr. Whipple and, calling out to him, asked if he would like to take Beal's place and make up a mixed doubles. Rather nervously Mr. Whipple replied that he did not play the game. His answer apparently decided them to give it up, for they all three left the courts and began slowly to make their way in the wake of Beal.

Left to himself and rather at a loose end, Mr. Whipple strolled off in the direction of the orchard. Here he found an under gardener at work, and getting into conversation with the man became so interested that he forgot all about the flight of time. He was rather surprised, therefore, to find when he began to return to the house that it was very nearly half past twelve. There was no sign of any one as he crossed the big lawn, but he noticed that the study windows were ajar and decided that he would drop in and see if his friend Hislop had finished his work.

Altering his direction, he had taken two steps when clearly to his ears came the sound of a shot! It was loud and distinct, and there was no mistaking it, and it came from the direction of the partly open windows of Robert Hislop's study!

Mr. Whipple started so violently and stopped so suddenly that he might have been shot himself.

Had Hislop been messing about with his revolver again, and had there been an accident? He felt his knees wobbling. At the sound of that sharp report all his uneasiness seemed to have become crystallized into one concentrated moment of horror.

He pulled himself together and began to run jerkily towards the terrace on to which the windows opened. He was ascending the stone steps when he heard the sound of excited voices, and crossing the broad flagstone reached the study just as Blanche Hislop and the girl Dorothy appeared at the windows of the drawing room.

'What was that noise?' asked Mrs. Hislop sharply.

Mr. Whipple shook his head helplessly.

'I don't know,' he mumbled. 'It sounded like a shot. It came from in here.'

He pulled open the French windows as he finished speaking and peered in, and the sight that he saw stamped itself for a long time afterwards on his memory.

Sprawling on the floor by the fireplace, his head in the fender, a trickle of blood running down his white face from a small, blue-rimmed hole in his forehead, was the unprepossessing Desmond Beal. Bending over him, a revolver still in his hand, was Robert Hislop!

3

THE RED CHESSMAN

Mr. Whipple, his small mouth agape, his throat suddenly dry, stared in speechless horror at the scene before him. He saw Robert Hislop look up sharply, and then he was pushed roughly aside as Mrs. Hislop thrust her way into the room.

'Robert!' she cried shrilly. 'What have you done?'

Her husband stared at her dazedly.

'I?' he mumbled. 'I haven't done anything. Something very serious has happened though. This fellow Beal has shot himself.'

Mr. Whipple heard a scream behind him, and looking round found that it had issued from the throat of the blonde girl.

'Oh!' she gasped. 'Is he dead?'

Robert Hislop looked towards her dazedly.

'I don't know,' he answered slowly. 'I'd

only just discovered him when you all arrived.'

He laid the revolver he had been holding down on the desk and bent over the prone figure of Beal. There was a long silence while he unfastened the man's coat and felt for his heart. Presently he looked up and his face was grave

'Yes, he's dead,' he said, and the words were spoken in such a low tone that they were barely audible. 'We'd better telephone for a doctor at once.'

'And the police!' The words left Mr. Whipple's lips before he could prevent them, and Blanche Hislop turned towards him quickly.

He was shocked at the change in her, for her face had suddenly grown haggard and old-looking.

'Is that, necessary?' she said. Her voice was harsh and edgy and there was an undercurrent of fear in it.

'I'm afraid it's very necessary,' answered Mr. Whipple almost apologetically, as though it was entirely his fault that it should be so. 'Unless you notify the police of this — this tragic occurrence you will get into serious trouble you know.'

'Whipple's right, dear,' said Hislop, nodding. 'Of course the police must be sent for.'

The sound of the shot had apparently been heard by Carol Linden and Geoffrey Ryman, for they appeared at the door of the study at that moment, accompanied by the startled butler, Droxford. Hislop cut short their excited and curious questions and shepherded them out into the hall, closing the door behind him.

'Oh, isn't it dreadful!'

The words were whispered into Mr. Whipple's ear, the breath of the speaker tickling the back of his neck, much to his annoyance, and he found the blonde girl, her face a pasty grey, at his elbow.

'I feel as though I am going to be sick!'

Mrs. Hislop, who had been staring at the dead man with a peculiar fascination, dragged her eyes away and swung round on her friend.

'If you feel upset you'd better go,' she said curtly. 'I'll take you into the drawing room.' She went over to the girl and almost pushed her out through the

French windows.

Mr. Whipple, left alone with the sprawling thing by the fireplace, glanced about him uneasily, and discovered that his feelings at that moment were a curious mixture. He was horrified at this proximity to sudden and violent death, but at the same time tremendously excited. Over and above his horror and the shock he had experienced was an overwhelming and intense curiosity, for Mr. Whipple was by no means assured that the dead man had committed suicide as suggested by Robert Hislop. Indeed, he was almost completely convinced that he had done nothing of the kind, and if this suggestion of suicide was eliminated then the only other alternative was — murder!

Mr. Whipple found his lips forming the word, and shuddered. It was one thing to read about such things in the comfort and security of his own home, but quite another matter to be faced with the reality, for if this was murder he was very vitally concerned.

The picture of Robert Hislop cleaning his revolver in the dead of night came unbidden into his mind, and was followed by the equally vivid picture of Robert Hislop bending over the body of the dead man with that same revolver in his hand. Mr. Whipple's eyes strayed to the sinister weapon that still lay where Hislop had put it down on the edge of the desk.

His memory conjured up the words he had heard Desmond Beal speak to an unknown listener in the garden on the previous evening while he had been dressing for dinner. 'I'm not going to be put off any longer, that's final. Either you come across with the money or I spill the beans. I'll give you till midday tomorrow and not a moment later.'

Supposing these words to have been addressed to Robert Hislop they supplied a reason for his at least wishing to ensure Beal's silence. There was no doubt of the threat they had conveyed Beal had been resorting to blackmail and the person he had blackmailed had preferred this means of silencing him to paying over the money he had demanded. The question was, was this person Robert Hislop or someone else?

Mr. Whipple was concerned and perplexed. When the police came it would be his duty to tell them all he knew. On the other hand, if he did he would be practically responsible for the arrest of his friend.

It was an extremely difficult position and it bothered him tremendously. He was very fond of Robert Hislop but if he had shot this man Beal then justice demanded that he should pay the penalty. Mr. Whipple had no pity for the victim. Beal had been of a type that he heartily disliked, and he considered blackmail, rightly, as the meanest of crimes. But at the same time murder was murder, and even blackmailers could not be killed with impunity.

'Dear me,' he murmured to himself, shaking his head. 'It's really going to be very awkward, very awkward indeed.'

He blinked, pulling nervously at his lower lip in his distress and was still doing so when Robert Hislop returned.

'The police and the doctor are on their way,' announced his friend as he came in, and then with a worried frown: 'This is going to be rather an unpleasant business, Whipple.'

Mr. Whipple nodded in agreement. No one realized more than he how unpleasant it might be.

'I'm afraid it is,' he said sorrowfully.

'If the fellow was set on committing suicide he might have chosen somewhere else to do it,' muttered Hislop with a grimace of distaste at the figure in the fireplace. 'And he might have chosen some other weapon than my revolver.'

Mr. Whipple was silent. It seemed to him that his friend was forcing home the fact that it was a case of suicide with undue insistence.

'Where were you when the shot was fired?' he asked diffidently.

'Upstairs in my bedroom,' replied Hislop. 'I came down at once and found him where he is now with the pistol by his side.'

'You — you didn't meet anyone on the staircase or in the hall?' enquired Mr. Whipple.

The other shook his head.

'No,' he answered. 'I met nobody.'

No one in the hall or on the staircase, no one on the terrace outside or I should have seen them, thought the worried Mr. Whipple. Really this is dreadful. If the man was murdered, as I think he was, Hislop is apparently the only person who could have done it! Aloud he said hesitantly:

'How long were you away from this room?'

'Not more than ten minutes,' was the answer. 'When I left you I came in here to write some letters that I wanted to catch the midday post. I finished them and gave them to Droxford to send to the pillar-box. After that I thought I'd have a shot at a chess problem that had beaten me once or twice before.'

He waved a hand towards the desk and Mr. Whipple saw that on the blotting pad was a chessboard set with one or two pieces.

'I managed to work it out,' continued Hislop, 'and then I remembered that my wife had asked me to look at a clock of hers which had gone wrong the night before. It had stopped at half-past twelve, and since it was a chiming clock and it's very easy to upset the chiming mechanism I had arranged to put it right at half-past twelve today. There was nothing very much the matter with it. I got it going, and then went along to my bedroom and I'd just reached it when I heard the sound of the shot.'

Mr. Whipple rubbed his chin nervously and peered at the chessboard. Although he was not then thinking about the game he subconsciously took in the position of the pieces, and something about them worried him. He looked again more closely.

'Surely,' he murmured, his eyes still on the board, 'there is something wrong with this problem? It's impossible to solve it without the red queen.'

'Of course, it is,' said Hislop impatiently. 'The red queen is the most important piece.'

'Well, where is it?' said Mr. Whipple.

'It's there, isn't it?' said his friend. 'It was anyway, when I left the room.'

Mr. Whipple looked at the desk and the board and peered into the box in which the chessmen were kept, but there was no sign of the red queen. He mentioned this fact, and Robert Hislop shrugged his shoulders.

'Well, it doesn't matter very much,' he remarked. 'We've got a more important problem before us than a missing chessman.'

But Mr. Whipple was methodical-minded, and the absence of the red queen disturbed him. He wondered if it had rolled onto the floor, and, stooping, peered under the desk. But there was no sign of it, and he was on the point of giving up his search when something about the dead man's right hand attracted his attention. He looked closer and saw that he had not been mistaken. Between the fingers of that clenched hand was a glimpse of red.

'It looks to me,' he said softly, straightening up and turning towards Hislop, 'as if the problem of the missing chessman and the death of this man Beal are connected.'

Hislop, who had been staring unsee-ingly out of the window, swung round.

'What do you mean?' he asked sharply.

'The red queen is in his hand,' answered Mr. Whipple gently. 'If you look carefully you can see it between the fingers. Now what is it doing there?'

Hislop came quickly over to his side and was stooping down when Mr. Whipple touched him gently on the arm.

'I wouldn't disturb it if I were you,' he cautioned. 'I should leave it where it is until after the police have seen it.'

4

FACTS

The police, in the persons of an inspector and a sergeant, arrived a few minutes later and were accompanied by a doctor. Inspector Blane, a thick-set, jovial man who might, from his brick-red face and sandy slither of side whiskers, have been a farmer, listened gravely while Robert Hislop told briefly what had happened and which was to all intents and purposes a repetition of what he had already told Mr. Whipple.

'It's your opinion the poor gentleman committed suicide, eh, sir?' asked the inspector when Hislop concluded, and the other nodded.

'It is,' he declared. 'I don't see what else it could have been — unless, of course, it was an accident.'

'You mean he might have been examining the revolver and set it off?' said

Blane, pursing his lips. 'Well, it's possible, I've heard of such cases — '

'But this isn't one of 'em!' The interruption came from the thin-faced doctor who was kneeling beside the body conducting his examination. 'This was no accident, Blane. It was deliberate, and I'm not so sure it was suicide, either!'

The inspector turned sharply, and Mr. Whipple, who had been nervously expecting to hear something of the sort, held his breath and glanced quickly at Robert Hislop.

The effect of the doctor's words on his friend was startling. His healthy colour receded as though it had been wiped from his face by an invisible sponge. His mouth drooped open, and he looked the picture of startled astonishment.

'What do you mean?' he gasped, and the words were jerked out hoarsely.

'What I say!' snapped the doctor. 'I don't think this was either an accident or suicide. It looks to me very like murder!'

The ominous word sent a thrill through his listeners, even Mr. Whipple, who had been expecting nothing else.

'On what do you base your statement, Doctor?' asked the inspector. His tone was matter of fact and phlegmatic but his eyes showed his excitement.

'On several things,' replied the doctor. 'First, you can discount accident by the nature of the wound. There is considerable powder blackening round it and rather bad singeing, which shows that the shot was fired not less than a foot away. It is hardly likely that any sane man would have held a loaded revolver so close to his head.'

Mr. Whipple nodded to himself in agreement with the doctor's argument.

'I see what you mean,' said the inspector slowly. 'But that doesn't preclude suicide.'

'No,' said the doctor, 'but the position of the wound makes it very unlikely.'

So he *has* seen that, thought Mr. Whipple a little triumphantly, for t had been one of the things he himself had noticed.

'The bullet entered the skull in the exact centre of the forehead,' went on the doctor, 'and followed a direct course, emerging at the back of the head on a level with the top of the ears It travelled in a perfectly straight line, for the exit hole is exactly opposite the entrance hole.'

'That's very interesting,' said the inspector looking at him doubtfully as he paused, 'But I don't quite see — '

'How it affects the issue?' finished the doctor. 'Well I'll tell you. If it was a case of suicide why did the man go out of his way to shoot himself in such a remarkably difficult manner? The attitude must have twisted his wrists most uncomfortably. Just try pointing your forefinger in a perfectly straight line at the middle of your forehead and you'll see what I mean.'

The inspector tried, and there was no doubt about the constraint of his attitude. Again Mr. Whipple nodded approvingly, and metaphorically patted himself on the back. His own conclusions had been confirmed.

'You see,' said the doctor triumphantly, 'and with the revolver in his hand it would have been even more difficult.'

'But not impossible,' put in Robert Hislop, but his voice was troubled. 'He *could* have done it.'

'Oh, he could have done it,' said the doctor a little impatiently, 'but why should he? It would have been far easier and just as effective to put the pistol to his right temple, and much more natural.'

'There's certainly something in what you say, Doctor,' grunted Inspector Blane. 'But it isn't really conclusive, is it?'

The doctor shrugged his shoulders.

'That's for you to decide,' he said. 'I'm merely giving you my opinion.'

'It must have been suicide,' muttered Hislop. 'Any other supposition is ridiculous. Who could have shot him if he didn't shoot himself?'

Inspector Blane rubbed his chin; clearly he was a rather puzzled man.

'I'm afraid, after what the doctor's pointed out, sir,' he said uncomfortably, 'I shall have to take every possibility into consideration.'

'Oh, quite right, Inspector,' said Hislop, 'but I assure you there is no one in my household or among my guests who would be likely to commit murder.'

'Would you mind,' said Mr. Whipple diffidently, 'would you mind, Doctor, looking at his right hand?'

The doctor eyed him with raised eyebrows.

'His right hand?' he echoed. 'Why — ?' He dropped his gaze. 'Oh, I see what you mean. He's holding something.'

'A chessman — the red queen,' murmured Mr. Whipple.

The doctor gently prised the dead fingers loose and the carved ivory chessman dropped onto the rug. The inspector picked it up and looked at it with a puzzled frown.

'Funny sort of thing to be in his hand,' he remarked.

'Very funny,' said the doctor thoughtfully. 'Very helpful all the same.'

'How?' asked Blane quickly.

'Was Mr. Beal left-handed or right-handed?' enquired the doctor.

'Right-handed.' It was Hislop who answered.

'Then there is your conclusive proof that he didn't commit suicide,' said the doctor decisively. 'To do so he would have had to fire the shot, drop the revolver and pick up this chess piece, and with a wound like that he couldn't possibly have done it.'

An uneasy silence followed his words. The inspector, still holding the red chessman in his thick fingers, was staring at it as though expecting to receive inspiration from the little carved piece of ivory. Mr. Whipple, troubled and uneasy, looked through his thick glasses at Robert Hislop, let his gaze wander from him to the doctor, and finally peered at the inspector as that gentleman raised his head.

'It looks very much as though we shall have to work on the assumption that this crime is murder, sir,' he announced gravely, addressing Hislop.

'It's incredible,' muttered Hislop. 'There must be a mistake somewhere.'

'If there is we shall probably find it, sir,' said the inspector. He threw off his air of troubled abstraction and became brisk and businesslike.

Setting the chessman down on the

desk, he stepped to the door and called to his sergeant, whom he had left in the hall. The man came, and took up his position just inside the doorway.

'Now, sir,' said the inspector producing a notebook from his breast pocket, 'I should be glad first of all, if you would give me the names of everyone in the house, including the servants.'

Robert Hislop hesitated for the fraction of a second and then complied. The inspector wrote them down carefully, and, when he had finished, read over his list aloud.

'Is that everyone, sir?' he asked, and after a moment's thought Hislop nodded. 'Take this, Neller.' Blane tore the page out of his notebook and held it out to the sergeant. 'None of these people is to leave under any excuse whatever until I've seen them. You understand?'

The man nodded.

'Be as tactful as you can, but don't let any of them leave the house,' added the inspector, and Neller nodded again and withdrew. When he had gone the inspector rose to his feet. 'You say the bullet passed right through the dead man's head, Doctor?' he asked.

'Right through,' said the doctor curtly.

'Then it ought to be somewhere in the room,' muttered the inspector, and began a search of the study.

But there was no sign of the spent bullet.

'That's funny,' said Blane when his futile search was over. 'What could have happened to it?'

The French windows were partly open.' Mr. Whipple made his suggestion apologetically. 'Isn't it possible, Inspector, that it passed through — '

'Out into the garden,' broke in the inspector. 'That's about what happened. Thank you, sir. I expect you're right. I'll have a search made later.' He took out his handkerchief and gingerly picked up the revolver. 'You found this lying beside the body, sir?' he turned to Hislop.

'Yes,' was the reply.

'It's a pity you picked it up,' murmured Blane. 'Would you mind showing me exactly where it lay?'

Without a word Hislop went over to

the fireplace and indicated a spot on the rug about three feet away from the body.

'Thank you, sir,' said the inspector. 'This revolver is your property I understand?'

Hislop nodded.

'Where do you usually keep it?'

'Here.' Hislop pointed to the middle drawer of the desk.

'I see that with the exception of one shot it's fully loaded. Do you usually keep it loaded?'

'Well no. Not as a general rule,' said Hislop reluctantly.

'When did you load it last then, sir?' asked Blane.

'Last night.'

The answer evidently surprised the inspector, for he raised his eyebrows.

'Why did you suddenly decide to load this weapon last night, sir?' he enquired.

'I — I don't really know.'

Mr. Whipple noticed the confusion in his friend's voice with a sinking heart.

'Just an impulse, I suppose.'

'I see, sir,' said Blane, but it was obvious that he did nothing of the kind.

'Who else, besides yourself, knew that there was a revolver in your desk?'

'My wife knew and most of the servants I think.'

'What about your guests?'

'Some of them.'

'Which of them?'

'Miss Linden. She came to ask me for a stamp yesterday afternoon. I keep stamps in that drawer. She saw the revolver and made some laughing remark about it.'

'And it's quite likely she may have mentioned it to some of your other guest?'

'Yes, quite likely.'

The inspector noted the answer and rubbed the side of his nose. There was a short silence while he stared with knitted brows at his notebook. Then he looked up.

'Now, I should like you to tell me, sir, all you know about the dead man,' he said.

5

QUESTIONS

The information that Robert Hislop was able to give concerning the dead man was of the slenderest. He had met Desmond Beal three years before at Biarritz while he and his wife were over there on a holiday. The man had made himself pleasant and they had become friendly. The three of them had returned to England together and after that they had seen a good deal of Beal.

So far as his private life was concerned Hislop was completely ignorant. Beyond the fact that he lived in a service flat in Ryder Street, St. James's, and always appeared to have plenty of money, he knew nothing about him at all.

Inspector Blane was obviously disappointed. He tapped on his teeth with the end of his pencil — a most irritating habit thought Mr. Whipple disapprovingly

— and stared at the open notebook before him.

'Do you know whether he had any relations living?' he asked presently.

'I've never heard him mention any,' answered Hislop.

'Was he married?'

'Not to my knowledge.' Hislop shook his head. 'He may have been. He was a very reticent man, not given to talking much about his private affairs.'

'Supposing this to have been murder then,' said the inspector, 'you can suggest no reason why any one should have committed the crime?'

Again Hislop shook his head, this time more emphatically.

'I can suggest no reason,' he replied. 'I still think you are making a mistake in regarding this as murder. I am convinced it was either an accident or suicide.'

Inspector Blane refrained from argument, and the doctor took advantage of the momentary silence to interpolate a remark.

'Well, you won't want me any more, Blane,' he said, 'so I'll be getting along, if you don't mind. I'm rather busy at the moment. I'll leave my report at the station this afternoon.'

'Right you are, Doctor,' said Blane, and with a curt nod to Mr. Whipple and Hislop the thin-faced man left them. 'Now, sir,' continued the inspector when he had gone. 'I think I should like to see some of the other people in the house, but I'd rather not interview them here, if it could be avoided. Not very pleasant for them while — ' He left the sentence unfinished but his eyes, straying to the dead man on the floor, clearly indicated what he meant.

'There's a small room just inside the front door,' said Hislop. 'Perhaps you'd like to use that?'

'Thank you, sir,' answered Blane, 'that's very kind of you.'

He got up, shut his notebook and put it back in his pocket. Crossing over to the French windows he closed them carefully and shot the bolt. Robert Hislop, waiting by the door, watched him impatiently.

'Nobody must be allowed in here,' explained the inspector. 'Is that a key on the inside of the door? I'll take it, if you don't mind, and lock the door after we go out.'

He suited the action to the word, and a moment later they were in the spacious hall, the door of the death room was locked and the key stowed away in one of the inspector's pockets. There was no sign of any of the household. With the exception of the sergeant, who was gloomily eyeing a large oil painting on the wall, the place was deserted. Hislop led the way over to a small room behind the big front door and ushered them in.

It was furnished cosily as a smoking-room and the inspector looked at it appreciatively. Pulling up a chair he seated himself at a small table, once more produced his notebook and consulted it. Presently he raised his eyes and looked at Mr. Whipple.

'I'll take your statement next, sir, if you please,' he said genially, and Mr. Whipple, who had been dreading this ordeal, waited expectantly.

'If you won't be requiring me, Inspector,' put in Hislop hastily, 'I should like to go and reassure my wife and my guests.'

'Certainly, sir,' said Blane. 'I've nothing more to ask you at the moment. I shall probably want to see you again later.'

With an expression of relief Hislop withdrew, and Mr. Whipple braced himself for the first of the barrage of questions he knew were coming. But he was granted a few moments' respite.

'If you'll just excuse me for a moment, sir,' said Blane, 'I'll have a word with my sergeant.'

He left the room swiftly and was gone for nearly two minutes. During the time he was left alone little Mr. Whipple tried unhappily to sort out his jumbled thoughts. He would have to say what he had overheard on the previous night while he had been dressing for dinner, but was it essential that he should state what he had seen during his excursion in the early hours of that morning? Strictly speaking it was but he decided to keep it to himself. He had no desire to make trouble for his friend, and if the police came to hear that Robert Hislop had sat up till half past two in the morning cleaning and loading the weapon that had killed Desmond Beal there might be serious trouble indeed.

Mr. Whipple salved his conscience by telling himself that after all the incident might have no bearing on the crime that followed. He was troubled, nevertheless, for he was a man of high principles, and this concealment was foreign to his nature.

Inspector Blane returned and took his place at the table.

'Sorry to keep you waiting,' he said apologetically, and took Mr. Whipple's name and address. 'Now, sir, I'd like to hear anything you can tell me that may help us to come to a conclusion about this business.'

He opened his notebook at a fresh page and eyed Mr. Whipple steadily. Mr. Whipple coughed nervously. This was not exactly the opening he had anticipated, and he was a little disconcerted.

'Well, really, I don't quite know — ' He reddened under the other's gaze and stammered confusedly.

The inspector compassionately came to his rescue.

'What I want to know, sir,' he said kindly, 'is whether you've noticed anything during your stay here that may have a bearing on this man's death?'

Mr. Whipple pulled himself together and hesitantly told the inspector what he had overheard. Blane listened interestedly.

'That's very important, sir,' he remarked, when Mr. Whipple stopped. 'Very important indeed. You're sure it was this man Beal who was speaking?'

'Positive!' declared Mr. Whipple, relieved that he had got the matter off his mind.

'And you've no idea to whom this threat was uttered?' asked Blane.

Mr. Whipple shook his head.

'No,' he answered. 'I've no idea at all.'

'Pity,' murmured the inspector, pursuing his lips. 'It would have helped a great deal if you could have told us that, sir.' He rubbed his chin and gently stroked one of his sandy whiskers. 'Would you mind repeating what you heard? I'd like to get the words exactly right.'

Mr. Whipple obligingly complied.

'I take it, sir,' went on the inspector when he had written them slowly down in his book, 'that you were not well acquainted with the dead man?'

'I met him for the first time yesterday,' said Mr. Whipple a little absently. He was debating whether he should inform the inspector of that other scrap of conversation he had overheard.

'Yes, sir?' Blane who was watching him, saw by his expression that there was something else coming, and prompted him. 'You've just thought of something, haven't you?'

'Well. I haven't exactly just thought of it,' said Mr. Whipple, 'but — Well, really, I seem to have done nothing but — I assure you I'm not in the habit of listening but I couldn't help hearing — '

'You heard something apart from the dead man's threat to someone unknown,' murmured the inspector gently.

'Well, yes, I did. Much later that night, just before I went to bed in fact.' Having committed himself Mr. Whipple drew a long breath and went through with it. He repeated the disjointed words used by Carol Linden.

'H'm!' Blane tapped his teeth with the end of his pencil, a habit of his apparently when he was thinking. 'The man she was speaking to — could it have been Beal?'

'It might have been. I don't know who it was,' said Mr. Whipple.

The inspector made a note in his book.

'Well, sir,' he said looking up, 'you've been very helpful. You've suggested a possible motive for someone wanting this fellow Beal out of the way, and it looks as though Miss Linden may be able to tell us something about that. There's nothing else you can remember, sir?'

'No, I'm afraid not,' said Mr. Whipple hastily, and wondered if he had lied convincingly.

'Then if you wouldn't mind going over again all that happened in the morning prior to your hearing the shot, I don't think I need trouble you any more for the moment.' Mr. Whipple once again went through his movements from the time he had come down to breakfast until the time he had heard the sound of the report while crossing the lawn.

At this point Blane stopped him.

'You didn't see anybody at all on the terrace, did you?' he asked.

Mr. Whipple shook his head. 'How long,' went on the inspector, 'was it between the time you heard the shot and the time you reached the windows of the study and saw Mr. Hislop and the dead man?'

Mr. Whipple considered.

'Somewhere in the region of three minutes,' he answered at length. 'Of course it's impossible for me to be accurate but — well, for some time after I heard the shot I was so startled that I couldn't move.'

Inspector Blane nodded indulgently.

'Quite understandable, sir,' he said. 'It must have been a very great shock. Now I think — '

What he thought Mr. Whipple was never destined to know, for at that moment, following a preliminary tap, the sergeant entered quickly. His large face was flushed and excited and he carried in his hand a crumpled piece of paper.

'I thought I'd better bring you this at once, sir,' he said. 'I found it in Mr. Hislop's dressing gown pocket.'

He laid the paper in front of the inspector, and Mr. Whipple, who was standing near the table, was able to make out the scrawled pencil message:

'Remember, twelve-thirty tomorrow is my limit. I shall not wait a moment after that time.'

The inspector's brows drew together as he read the note, then he looked up sharply.

'You found this in Hislop's dressing gown pocket, did you?' he asked, and the sergeant nodded.

'Yes, sir,' he replied. 'Hanging up behind the door of his bedroom.'

Once more Inspector Blane's pencil tapped an irregular tattoo on his teeth.

'I'll have a word with Mr. Hislop about this,' he said presently. 'Go and find him, Neller, and ask him to step in here for a moment.'

6

ARREST

Robert Hislop came promptly, looking, or so Mr. Whipple thought, a little worried and anxious.

'You want me, Inspector?' he asked.

Blane raised his eyes from the note that was spread on the table in front of him.

'I do, sir,' he answered, and there was a subtle difference in his tone, a hardness underlying the smooth geniality. 'I should like you to tell me what you know about — this.' He picked up the paper and held it out suddenly, with a movement that was almost dramatic.

Hislop took it, peered at it, and drew down his eyebrows.

'I don't know anything about it,' he said. 'Where did you get it?'

'It's the dead man's writing isn't it?' The inspector ignored the question.

Hislop nodded and his expression was puzzled.

'Yes, it's Beal's writing,' he replied. 'But I don't understand it. Who was this written to?'

'You've never seen it before?' asked Blane, his eyes fixed steadily on the other's face.

'No, of course I haven't,' said Hislop. 'Why should I?'

'Because it was found in the pocket of your dressing gown,' answered the inspector.

'My — my dressing gown?' echoed Hislop incredulously. 'How the devil did it get there?'

'That's what I should like you to explain, sir,' said Blane.

Mr. Whipple saw the amazement on his friend's face change to doubt and consternation as he realized the full significance of this discovery.

'I can't explain it, Inspector,' he said quietly. 'For the simple reason that I know nothing about it.'

'This note was not written to you?' said the inspector.

Hislop shook his head.

'Most certainly not,' he said.

'Then what was it doing in your dressing gown?' Blane's question was curt, and the hardness that Mr. Whipple had previously noticed had slightly increased.

'I haven't the least idea,' answered Hislop. 'Somebody must have put it there.'

'I quite realize that, sir,' said the inspector.

'What I mean is,' said Hislop hastily, 'somebody apart from myself.'

There was disbelief on the inspector's face and he pursed his lips.

'Then you affirm, sir,' he said after a pause, 'that this note was never written to you, that you haven't seen it before, and that if it was found in the pocket of your dressing gown somebody else must have put it there?'

'Yes,' answered Hislop.

'Can you suggest then,' said Blane, 'who would be likely to do such a thing?'

'No, I can't,' replied Hislop.

The inspector fiddled with his pencil.

'Did you hold a conversation with the dead man last night?' he continued, after a short silence, 'during which he used the words, 'I am not going to be put off any longer, that's final. Either you come across with the money or I spill the beans. I'll give you till midday tomorrow and not a moment later.' '

'No!' retorted Híslop. 'Look here, Inspector, what are you getting at?'

'I'm trying to get at the truth, sir,' said Blane. 'Evidence has reached me which throws a different complexion on this business. It seems certain, from what I've been able to gather, that this man Beal was threatening someone in the house with the object of extorting money. In other words he was resorting to blackmail.'

If Hislop was acting he was doing it very well, thought Mr. Whipple, who was watching his friend intently, for he looked the picture of astonishment at the inspector's words.

'Blackmail!' he repeated. 'I can't believe it. It sounds ridiculous.'

'It may, sir, but it's true all the same,'

said Blane. 'Now this note that was found in your dressing gown pocket fits in with the words which Beal was heard to utter, and supplies a motive for somebody wishing to kill him.'

'And you think that somebody was me?' said Hislop.

The inspector made a deprecatory movement with his hands.

'I don't think anything at the moment, sir,' he said evasively. 'I'm merely collecting evidence. Naturally, since this note was found in your dressing gown pocket I turned to you for an explanation of it.'

'Well, I'm afraid I can't give you one,' said Hislop. 'I've never seen that note before, and I have no idea how it got where you found it.'

Blane was obviously not satisfied. It was fairly evident to Mr. Whipple that he did not believe Hislop, and taking everything into consideration Mr. Whipple could hardly blame him. He found it difficult to believe his friend himself. Everything pointed to the fact that it was Hislop who had fired the fatal shot that had killed Desmond Beal. The man had known something which Hislop didn't want made public property, and had taken this method of silencing him. But, thought Mr. Whipple, how could he have been so incredibly stupid, shooting him in broad daylight, letting himself be found with the revolver in his hand, and leaving that note in the pocket of his dressing gown. Perhaps he had been going to destroy it later and had found no opportunity for doing so.

His heart was heavy, for he was very fond of the bluff retired grocer, whose little shop had been next to his own. He was in an unpleasant position, and he seemed to realize it, for worried lines had appeared on his face and it was almost haggard when he left the little smoking-room at the inspector's dismissal.

'Dear me,' Mr. Whipple ventured in his distress to address Blane as he made a note in his book. 'I hope you don't — that is, I really don't think — It's — er — impossible to suppose — ?'

'Yes, sir?' said the inspector kindly as

Mr. Whipple floundered badly.

'You — you don't suspect Mr. Hislop?' With a great effort Mr. Whipple got the words out.

The inspector looked grave.

'Well, sir, it looks very peculiar, doesn't it?' he said.

Mr. Whipple had to confess that it did look very peculiar.

'But — really!' he gasped feebly. 'I've known Hislop for some years — I should never — the last person I should have thought — '

Blane shook his head slowly.

'You never can tell in these kinds of cases,' he said. 'Blackmail's a nasty business, and I can't say my sympathy isn't with the person who bumped this fellow off. But the law's the law and I've got my duty to do.'

'Then you do — you do think — ' began Mr. Whipple.

'I think,' interrupted the inspector blandly, 'that I'd better get on with my job, if you don't mind, sir.'

Mr. Whipple accepted the rebuke in silence.

Carol Linden was sent for, and came. Sullen, but beneath her sullenness, half frightened, she answered the inspector's questions shortly.

She had been in the dining room when she had heard the shot, drinking a gin and ginger beer. There had been nobody with her, but when she came out to see what the noise was she had met Geoffrey Ryman in the hall. Concerning the words, which Mr. Whipple had heard her use on the previous night, she refused to give any explanation at all. The matter had been a private one and had had no connection whatever with Beal, and therefore was none of the inspector's business. She was irritable and bad tempered, and hinted that the quicker she could leave East Gables the better she'd like it.

Blane let her go and sent for Ryman. He came, a nervous and uneasy man. At the time he had been startled by the report of the pistol he had been in his room, filling his case with cigarettes. He had come down and in the hall had met Carol Linden just coming out of the dining room. He had seen nobody else, except Droxford, the butler, who joined them as they reached the door of the study, from the direction of the servants' stair. Ryman was agitated and answered the inspector's questions jerkily.

Droxford, the butler, had been talking to the kitchen maid when the report had brought him to the hall. He confirmed Carol Linden and Ryman's statement that they had met outside the study door.

Blanche Hislop, coldly composed, stated that she had been in the drawing room talking to Miss Wier, — so that was the blonde girl's name, thought Mr. Whipple — when the muffled sound of the shot had reached her from the next room. She had thought at first that something had fallen down, and had come out onto the terrace where she had met Mr. Whipple.

None of the people at East Gables appeared to know anything more about Beal than was already known.

Dorothy Wier, the blonde-haired girl, confirmed Mrs. Hislop's statement, but could offer no other information.

The remainder of the servants were

questioned, but their evidence added nothing to the inspector's meagre stock of facts.

It all looked very black against Hislop, thought Mr. Whipple sorrowfully, for apparently he was the only person who could have fired the shot. Blanche Hislop and Dorothy Wier supplied each other with an alibi. Droxford had been talking to the kitchen-maid at the time, and Carol Linden, Geoffrey Ryman and Robert Hislop were the only three people who had no one to confirm their movements.

The inspector conducted a search of the dead man's room, but found nothing of importance, and finally took his departure, carrying with him the revolver.

In spite of the brightness of the summer's day an air of gloom hung about the house. No one had thought about lunch and no one felt very much inclined to eat. A scratch meal of sandwiches was provided late in the afternoon, and, this was partaken of for the most part in silence.

At five o'clock Inspector Blane returned,

accompanied by a constable.

Mr. Whipple, who was in the hall when they arrived, heard him ask for Robert Hislop, and his heart sank. His apprehension was justified. The revolver which Blane had carried away had been tested for fingerprints, and the only ones found on it were Hislop's. Ten minutes after the inspector's second arrival at the house he was under arrest, charged with the wilful murder of Desmond Beal, and warned that anything he might say would be taken down and later used in evidence at his trial.

7

MR. WHIPPLE IS NOT SATISFIED

The shock of her husband's arrest completely prostrated Blanche Hislop, and left Mr. Whipple in a state of unutterable dejection. Although the evidence against his friend seemed overwhelming and he had foreseen his possible arrest Mr. Whipple could not bring himself to believe that he was guilty. And yet, if Robert Hislop had not fired that fatal shot, who had? Only two other people could have had the opportunity, Carol Linden or Geoffrey Ryman.

Mr. Whipple wandered miserably round the grounds of East Gables trying to hit on something that would suggest a line of enquiry that might benefit his friend. Two things in the chain of evidence against Hislop worried him. One was the red chessman found in the dead man's clenched hand, and the other was that a careful search conducted by Inspector Blane had failed to bring to light the spent bullet. That it had not been found was peculiar, but not extraordinary, when one came to think, as Mr. Whipple was convinced that it had sped through the open windows of the study after passing through Beal's head. At the same time it should have been found somewhere on the broad expanse of lawn, for the resistance of a man's head was considerable, and the velocity of the bullet must have been considerably decreased by the obstacle. And yet although every inch of the smooth grass had been subjected to a close scrutiny there was no sign of it.

The fact that it was not there might be very important indeed, although Mr. Whipple could not quite see how. But what was certainly important was the red queen in Beal's hand, for although he puzzled his brains Mr. Whipple could find no reason for it being there. At the very instant he had been shot Beal must have grabbed the chessman. According to the doctor's evidence it had not been put in his hand after death, and death had occurred so quickly after the firing of the shot that the action of his picking up the chessman and the pulling of the trigger must have been almost simultaneous; But why? The natural action of a man faced with a loaded revolver is to make some attempt to evade the bullet, but this could not have been Beal's motive for picking up the red queen. Had it been a paperweight or something heavy it would have been a different matter, but the chessman could not, by any stretch of imagination, be regarded as a missile that Beal had intended to hurl at his attacker.

Mr. Whipple sighed. Perhaps he was attaching a great deal too much importance to it. Men on the point of death did strange things.

In one of his favourite books it would, of course, have formed the vital clue to the identity of the murderer. But such things did not always work out the same in real life. Perhaps Beal had stumbled forward and grabbed the chesspiece unconsciously.

It was curious all the same. In fact the whole thing was curious. There had been a ring of truth in Hislop's voice when he had denied all knowledge of the note, and the expression on his face when he had heard of it had certainly been one of astonishment. Had he really been surprised at the finding of the note in his dressing gown pocket?

Mr. Whipple stopped under an ancient oak tree, took off his glasses and polished them vigorously. Could the note have been put where it had been found by the real murderer for the purpose of throwing suspicion on Hislop? Had the killer of Beal worn gloves when he, or she, had fired, knowing that the result would be that only Hislop's fingerprints would be found on the pistol? Mr. Whipple put on his glasses again and wiped his forehead. Was he seeking a difficult explanation when a perfectly simple one lay before his eyes? Had his hobby blunted his sense of values? Was he trying to infuse into real life the element that made his books so interesting?

And yet that red chessman in the dead man's hand!

Mr. Whipple's mind kept returning to that again and again. It was so extraordinary that it really must mean something. And quite suddenly he came to a decision. He would go back to town and consult his friend, Inspector Gallers. On more than one occasion his suggestions had been useful to that official, now Gallers could make himself useful in his turn.

Mr. Whipple returned to the house, borrowed a timetable and looked up a train. There was one at seven twenty-five, and he arranged with the butler to be driven to the station.

Blanche Hislop came down the stairs just as he was leaving, her face pale and dark marks below her eyes.

'Surely you're not going, Mr. Whipple,' she said anxiously. 'I wanted to have a talk to you about — about Robert.'

'I — I'm afraid I must go up to town,' said Mr. Whipple nervously. 'But I shall not be gone very long. I hope to return either tonight or tomorrow morning'

She looked at him, her large eyes burning.

'Something must be done,' she said, 'to prevent this dreadful mistake. You've known Robert all his life, you can't think he did this awful thing!'

Mr. Whipple moistened his lips uncomfortably.

'I — well, of course — the evidence — '

'The evidence!' she broke in scornfully. 'You, a friend of Robert's to talk about evidence!'

Mr. Whipple shuffled his feet and rubbed his small, plump hands together unhappily.

'I — I was only going to say,' he mumbled, 'that — er — in face of — the police could do nothing else.'

'But we can do something!' she cried. 'We must do something! I've telephoned to Robert's lawyer and he's coming tomorrow.'

'That was a very wise precaution,' said Mr. Whipple approvingly. 'He will no doubt be of great assistance — '

'But he can't do much,' said Blanche

Hislop despairingly. 'He can only advise. What we want is to find out the truth of this matter. Don't you see, if Robert didn't kill this man, and he didn't, the only thing that can help him is to find the person who did.'

'Yes — yes, of course,' Mr. Whipple nodded, glancing surreptitiously at his watch. 'Of course. In fact I — well, it — er — struck me that — I have a friend who lives next door to me — an inspector in Scotland Yard — '

She grasped his meaning from this somewhat incoherent statement.

'And you're going up to town to consult him?' she asked eagerly.

'That was my intention,' said Mr. Whipple. 'Of course he can't — nothing really to do with him, you see, unless the local police — er — consult the Yard. But he may be able to suggest — '

'Yes, yes, go and see him,' she said, seizing his arm so tightly that he blinked. 'Do everything you can. We must get Robert out of this horrible mess.'

She almost pushed him down the steps to the waiting car and he stumbled into the back seat with a sigh of profound relief.

Mr. Whipple was constitutionally nervous of women and emotional women scared him out of his wits.

He caught his train with barely a quarter of a minute to spare. Throughout the journey — he had a first class compartment to himself — he concentrated on this problem, which had irrupted into the peaceful course of his life.

The train was drawing into Waterloo when he sat up with a jerk. A sudden incredible idea had flashed through his mind; an illusive memory of that dinner on the evening he had come to East Gables, and linked with it was the red queen in Desmond Beal's dead hand. Was that the explanation for the presence of the chessman?

It seemed wildly absurd; an impossible theory, and yet —

'Dear me,' muttered Mr. Whipple shaking his head, as he hurriedly prepared to alight. 'How dreadful if it should be true. Really, I ought to go back to Chittering tonight!'

8

THE FIGURE IN THE STUDY

Mr. Whipple had a long chat with Inspector Gallers, and indeed, did most of the talking, for the Scotland Yard detective was a man who habitually said very little. He listened more or less indulgently to what the little man had to tell him, and when Mr. Whipple timidly advanced the theory that had come to him in the train he smiled.

'It does credit to your imagination, Mr. Whipple,' he said slowly in his ponderous way, 'but really, I think it's a bit far-fetched.'

Mr. Whipple looked disappointed.

'Do you?' he asked. 'I can think of no other way to account for that chessman.'

Gallers reached out his hand picked up the whisky and soda with which his friend had provided him and sipped it appreciatively.

'Must it be accounted for?' he said. 'Aren't you rather mixing up all these books you read' — he waved his hand towards the closely packed shelves — 'with real life? When you come across something like that in a book you know it's put there for a purpose, otherwise it wouldn't have been mentioned. But in real life it may just be there, there may be no rhyme or reason for it.'

'But — it's such an unusual thing,' argued Mr. Whipple. 'There must be a reason why this man Beal should have died with the chessman in his hand.'

Inspector Gallers shook his head.

'In a book, yes,' he answered. 'In real life, no. It may just mean nothing at all. He may have grabbed it subconsciously. I don't know your friend, but it looks very much to me as if he did kill this fellow, and I think you're trying to find a roundabout explanation when Blane has already found a simple one.'

Mr. Whipple, who had been really elated with his new idea, felt his spirits somewhat dampened, but he was reluctant to relinquish his theory. His diffident arguments however, had no effect on the practical Gallers. He listened politely but sceptically.

'To prove your theory,' he said, when Mr. Whipple had exhausted himself trying to bring the other round to his way of thinking, 'you've got to show how the crime could have been committed. At the present moment you're suggesting an impossibility. Until you can show that it was possible it's not practical.'

'I know that,' agreed Mr. Whipple, 'I thought — I was hoping — with your varied experience that you might — perhaps suggest a line. You see, my theory also explains why the bullet wasn't found.'

But Inspector Gallers was not to be convinced. He promised, however, that the first thing on Monday morning he would institute the enquiries that Mr. Whipple had suggested, and telephone his friend the result, if any.

With this Mr. Whipple had to be content. He took leave of his friend, interviewed his housekeeper — a gaunt Scots woman who filled his timid soul with terror — and drove by taxi to Waterloo. He just succeeded in catching the last train to Godalming, and it was not until the train had gone out of the station that he remembered that he ought to have phoned to East Gables for the car to meet him. His mind had been so fully occupied that this detail had slipped his memory.

'Dear me,' thought Mr. Whipple disconsolately, 'unless I can pick up some form of conveyance I shall have to walk. It will be too late to phone from Godalming, everyone will be in bed.'

The train deposited him on Godalming platform at ten minutes to one, and he quickly discovered that any form of vehicle that would convey him to East Gables was as scarce as water in the Sahara.

It was ten miles to Chittering, and although the night was fine and warm Mr. Whipple did not relish the prospect. There was nothing for it, however, unless he stayed the night in Godalming, and so he made the best of a bad job and set out on his journey. As he walked along through the silent country a fresh complication occurred to him. By the time he reached East Gables it would be well after three, he was unused to walking and his pace was by no means a quick one. This meant that the house would be locked up.

Mr. Whipple took out his handkerchief and wiped his perspiring forehead.

'Really, it's going to be very awkward,' he murmured to himself. 'I shall have to knock up the servants.'

He began to wish that he'd stayed in London, and as he continued to tramp along, weary and a little footsore, without apparently appreciatively decreasing the distance between himself and his objective, his wish grew in intensity. His timid and retiring nature rebelled against having to arouse a sleeping house in order to gain admittance. Maybe, he thought hopefully, there will be a window unlatched.

He passed through the dark and sleeping village of Chittering as the clock in the old church struck three, and ascending the hill turned thankfully into the drive at East Gables, The tunnel of chestnuts was very dark, for the thickly growing trees met overhead and screened even the faint light from the stars. As he came round the bend in sight of the house he saw that it was in complete darkness. He had expected nothing else, but the sight increased his misgivings.

He paused irresolutely at the steps leading up to the porch and his whole being shuddered at the idea of disturbing that peaceful stillness by ringing the bell. Perhaps there was some means by which he could slip into the house without arousing its inmates.

He began to move towards the back, and subconsciously walked on tiptoe. He came to the lawn and in sight of the broad stone steps leading up to the terrace.

He was making his way towards these when a flicker of light attracted his attention and he stopped, peering towards the place where he had seen it with bated breath. It came again, the momentary flicker of a torch, and it came from Robert Hislop's study.

For a moment Mr. Whipple felt a chill of superstitious fear. That flickering light in the darkness of the night, shining intermittently from the windows of the room in which Desmond Beal had been done to death was peculiarly eerie. Did it emanate from the hand of a living person or —

Mr. Whipple mentally shook himself. Such thoughts were foolish, childish! There was nothing ghostly about an electric torch. Somebody was in the study. Mr. Whipple experienced a thrill of excitement. Who was it who was in that room, which death had visited, at this hour of the morning?

The prospect that he was on the verge of an important discovery thrilled him and set his heart beating fast.

Cautiously he crept towards the stone steps and began to ascend them, careful to make not the slightest sound. As he came onto the terrace he saw that the French windows of the study were now dark. It struck Mr. Whipple that he might have made some slight sound and that the person within the darkened room was staring out at him.

The idea made his flesh creep. There was something extraordinarily unnerving in the thought that behind those dark panes an eager face was pressed, staring out into the night, watchful and intent.

Mr. Whipple stooped in the shadow of the balustrade and, with his eyes fixed on the windows, waited. But apparently the person within had heard nothing, for in a few seconds the light flashed again, and from where he crouched the little man was able to look into the room, and saw that it came, as he had thought, from a torch held in the hand of a shadowy figure who was stooping down by the side of the fireplace. The light was very dim and neither the features nor the sex of the night visitant to Robert Hislop's study was identifiable. The person, whoever it was, seemed to be working at something and Mr. Whipple, tingling with curiosity that got the better of his apprehension, stole softly across the intervening stretch of flagstones with the intention of getting a closer view. In this he was doomed to disappointment for he was within a foot of the window when his shoe kicked a loose stone that he failed to notice in the darkness. It shot forward and hit the woodwork of the window with a noise that was so exaggerated in the stillness that it sounded like the explosion of a minor bomb.

Mr. Whipple drew in his breath with a gasp, but the mischief was done. Instantly the light within went out. He heard the soft click of a latch and the gentle closing of a door. The unknown person in Robert Hislop's study had taken alarm and gone.

9

GATHERING THE THREADS

Mr. Whipple woke late on that Sunday morning, and even when he had shaved, had his bath and dressed, he still felt tired. There had been no means of gaining admittance to the house except by the front door, and after a great deal of hesitation he had summoned up sufficient courage to ring the bell. Even then it had been nearly a quarter of an hour before a sleepy-eyed and slightly indignant Droxford had appeared in pyjamas and dressing gown and opened it for him.

The butler had tried to conceal his astonishment at the appearance of a guest at such an extraordinary hour, and Mr. Whipple had timorously apologized, explaining incoherently the reason for his arrival at this untimely hour. An explanation and an apology which Droxford accepted with dignified silence.

With his morning tea, came a note from Blanche Hislop saying that she was breakfasting in her room and would see Mr. Whipple later.

It was half-past ten when he made his way downstairs to the dining room and took his breakfast in solitary state. Geoffrey Ryman had had his an hour earlier and had gone for a walk. Carol Linden and the blonde girl were having theirs in their respective rooms. Mr. Whipple was not sorry. He had a great deal to think about, and over his leisurely meal he methodically sorted and pigeon-holed the various theories and ideas that were seething in his brain.

How did this person whom he had surprised in Hislop's study fit in with his previous theory?

Mr. Whipple cogitated on this for a long time, and discovered that the person fitted in very well. The reason for the visit in the dead of night had been an attempt to cover up the only clue that might lead to the identity of the real murderer.

Yes, that was it.

As he buttered his last piece of toast

and reached for the marmalade Mr. Whipple came to the conclusion that he must see the inside of the study at the first available opportunity. There were several things he had to do that day. He wanted, if possible, to have a word with Carol Linden, and quite a long conversation with Blanche Hislop. There was a question he wished to ask Inspector Blane also.

He drank his second cup of coffee, carefully wiped his mouth, and methodically brushed the crumbs from the knees of his trousers, rose to his feet and went out into the garden.

It was a lovely day, although a trifle too hot and oppressive, and Mr. Whipple strolled gently along the twisting paths as they wound their way between colourful flowerbeds, his mind still intent on his problem.

On his way back to the house he almost ran into Carol Linden. The girl came quickly out of a side path and nearly cannoned into him before he was aware of her approach. Although it was not Mr. Whipple's fault he apologized but she barely acknowledged his conciliatory words. With a muttered 'It doesn't matter,' she passed him and went on in the direction from whence he had come.

Mr. Whipple was shocked, not so much at her rudeness as at her appearance. Her face was haggard and white, and the redness of her eyelids was eloquent testimony that she had been crying. He shook his head as he continued on his way.

'Poor girl,' he said to himself. 'Poor, poor child! Well I suppose these things happen.'

He entered the house by the open windows of the drawing room, and had discovered the blonde girl, Dorothy Wier, curled up on a settee intently manicuring her fingernails. She gave him a smile of greeting and he quickly saw that if the shadow of death that hung over the house had depressed the rest of the inmates it had had no effect on the vivacious Miss Wier. She was as voluble as ever, and Mr. Whipple, who was anxious to extract an item of information from her, suffered her noisy chatter with exemplary patience.

When he left her, twenty minutes later to seek the telephone, he had added another fact to his steadily increasing stock.

Luckily, Inspector Blane was at the police station when Mr. Whipple got through.

'Er — I — I want to know,' said Mr. Whipple hesitantly, 'if you could enlighten me on two small points, Inspector.'

The inspector assured him that he would do his best.

'Er — when you examined the — the dead man's clothing,' went on Mr. Whipple, 'was — er — any portion of it singed or burned?'

'Now how did you know that, sir?' asked the surprised Blane. 'Did you notice it when we were all in the study?'

'Er — yes — I think I did,' lied Mr. Whipple, who had done nothing of the sort. 'So there is — er — a singed mark, Inspector?'

'There is,' admitted Blane. 'A slight burn on the leg of his trousers.'

'Thank you,' said Mr. Whipple gratefully. 'Thank you very much. And the revolver. Now could you inform me whether it is of the kind known as a hair trigger?'

'Yes, it is,' said the inspector. 'But — '

'Thank you. It's extremely kind of you,' said Mr. Whipple hastily, and rang off before the astonished police official could put the question that hovered on his lips.

He left the instrument breathing a little quickly, his eyes behind his thick spectacles gleaming with excitement. The wild and improbable theory which had come to him so suddenly in the train and which owed its genesis to the finding of the red queen in Desmond Beal's dead hand, was becoming less wild and less improbable. The more he thought of it and tested it with the facts in his possession the more he was convinced that he was right.

He met Blanche Hislop in the hall. She looked as if she hadn't slept, and Mr. Whipple, realizing the strain under which she was living, was not surprised. She questioned him eagerly concerning the result of his visit to London, and seemed disappointed that he had achieved no more. He learned that Robert Hislop's lawyer was coming down to lunch. and was rather pleased, for it was necessary that he should have a word or two with that legal gentleman.

Geoffrey Ryman came in from his walk at that moment and carted his hostess away for a stroll round the garden. Mr. Whipple was rather glad than otherwise to be alone, for he had still to find some means of examining the study. The door was locked and the French windows bolted, and it looked as if his curiosity concerning that spot near the fireplace, which had occupied the attention of the mysterious person during the night, was to be unappeased.

A piece of luck, however, gratified his desire.

The lock on the study door was old-fashioned, as were most of the locks in the house, and Mr. Whipple, after a tentative experiment discovered that the key of the drawing room fitted the lock of the study.

Assuring himself that he was unobserved, he transferred the key, opened the study door, and slipping inside relocked the door behind him.

With the exception of the fact that the sprawling figure of Desmond Beal no longer lay on the crumpled hearth rug, the room was in exactly the same condition as when he had last seen it.

The blood where the dead man's head had rested still stained the tiles of the fireplace.

Mr. Whipple averted his eyes hurriedly and tried to control the nausea that the sight evoked. Making up his mind not to look at that sinister stain, he went over and bending down carefully examined the spot where the night intruder had been so busy.

When he cautiously emerged from the death room, ten minutes later, relocked it, and put the key back in the drawing room door, he was in possession of all the truth.

Mr. Letten, Hislop's lawyer, arrived shortly before one: a big, stout, grey-haired man, to whom Mr. Whipple took a liking on sight.

After lunch he managed to get the man of law to himself.

'This is a very dreadful business about Hislop,' said Mr. Letten gravely, 'and his wife, too, poor little woman. She's as loyal as they make 'em, and won't hear of the possibility of her husband being guilty.'

'I think she's right,' murmured Mr. Whipple. 'I don't believe Robert is guilty.'

The lawyer gave him a quick glance.

'Any reason?' he said. 'Or just because you're an old friend?'

'Several reasons,' said Mr. Whipple. 'Would — would you mind telling me something — '

Before the lawyer could reply he put his question. Mr. Letten's bushy eyebrows rose.

'Why do you want to know that?' he asked curiously.

Mr. Whipple hesitated.

'Will you treat what I am going to tell you in strict confidence?' he said, and the lawyer was surprised by the gravity in his tone.

'Well that depends,' he answered cautiously. 'If you know anything definite that ought to be in possession of the police I'm afraid that I — '

'At the present moment,' broke in Mr. Whipple with a firmness that surprised himself, 'I know nothing definite. What I am about to tell you is — is merely an idea which certain facts that I have accumulated more or less makes permissible.'

He looked round him cautiously. They were strolling across the centre of the big lawn and there was no one in sight.

'Listen,' he said, and lowering his voice he began to talk. And he talked solidly for twenty minutes, during which time Mr. Letten listened, and as he listened the expression on his face changed from incredulity to amazement, and from amazement to a peculiar mingling of doubt and conviction.

'It sounds incredible!' he muttered, 'and yet, somehow I believe you may be right.'

For the first time in his life Mr. Augustus Whipple spoke decisively.

'I know I'm right!' he declared. 'The difficulty is how am I going to prove it?'

10

IN THE SUMMERHOUSE

After an interview later that afternoon with Robert Hislop at the police station at Godalming to which he had been taken, Mr. Letten returned to London, a grave, thoughtful, and if the truth must be told, a greatly worried man. His client had done nothing either to help him or himself.

'I can only say, Letten, that I didn't shoot the man,' he declared. 'The story I have told the police is the truth. There was no reason why I should want to kill Beal. I had nothing against him, and as for that note, I can't account for it. The whole thing's a ghastly mistake.'

The lawyer, fresh from the confidence of Mr. Whipple, thought it might be ghastly, but hardly a mistake. He kept this thought, however, to himself, for the little man had been most insistent that he should not divulge to any one his theories or suspicions. Mr. Whipple had no proof that would satisfy the law and he was diffident enough to recognize the possibility that he might not be able to obtain any. In that case he had no wish to raise hopes that might be dashed to the ground for lack of the material evidence the law demands.

That Sunday evening was one of the worst periods of time Mr. Whipple ever remembered having passed through. Retiring to his room early on the plea of a headache — he was becoming to his astonishment, a fluent liar — he pulled up a chair to the open window and wrestled with his problem of proof. And a very difficult problem he found it, for there was nothing he could bring forward in support of his theory. Not the tiniest shred of that material evidence which he so desired. He went over in his mind all the points on which he had based his incredible conviction. The red chessman in Beal's hand. The failure of the police to find the spent bullet. The slight singe on the dead man's trousers. That the revolver possessed a hair trigger, and a small hole in the wainscot near the fireplace in the study. A clever counsel would laugh these meagre facts to scorn.

Mr. Whipple had certainly seen with his own eyes somebody in the study preparing to stop that tiny hole, but he couldn't swear who that person was, although he himself knew only too well.

Huddled in his chair lie racked his brain for a solution. If only he had definite proof that Beal had been blackmailing the person he suspected and not Robert Hislop . . .

'Dear me!' Mr. Whipple exclaimed ten minutes later. 'How foolish of me. Of course that's it. Five dead goldfish. That is undoubtedly the solution.'

*   *   *

Immediately after breakfast on the following morning Mr. Whipple walked down to the village to put the first part of his plan into execution. The letter he had carefully prepared overnight he slipped into the pillar-box and entering the little post office ensconced himself in the telephone cabinet.

After some trouble he got through to Scotland Yard and presently found himself talking to Inspector Gallers.

'I want — that is I should like — er — be very much obliged if you — It's possible to give me great assistance,' said Mr. Whipple nervously, and explained with many pauses what it was he did want. 'You see,' he concluded a little breathlessly, 'you would carry more weight — er — they may not — I don't look sufficiently important — if you could manage it, perhaps about half-past eight or possibly nine — Oh, thank you. That is really very kind. Dear me, I'm extremely grateful.'

Mr. Whipple launched into a flood of thanks and came out of the telephone box mopping his streaming forehead.

If anything the day promised to be hotter than Sunday, but there were signs of a break. The air was heavy and oppressive and there was a tinge of copper in the stifling blue vault of the sky. The long heatwave looked as if it would break in a storm.

Mr. Whipple noticed the signs with uneasiness as he walked slowly back towards East Gables. Coming up the drive he met Carol Linden. She had completely ignored him throughout the previous day, and he was preparing to pass her with a polite 'good morning' when she stopped.

'How long do you think it will be before we are allowed to go?' she asked abruptly.

Mr. Whipple blinked at her and considered. He knew she was referring to Inspector Blane's orders that no one was to leave the house until permitted to do so by the police. Orders that he himself had forgotten when he made his hurried journey to London.

'I really couldn't say,' he answered. 'I should think — not very long now. Possibly after the inquest.'

'When is that?' she demanded.

'Wednesday, I believe,' said Mr. Whipple, who knew very well that it was Wednesday, because he had been told so by the inspector. 'We shall of course, receive a subpoena.'

'Wednesday?' echoed the girl in dismay. 'We've got to be cooped up here till then?'

'I'm afraid we have,' agreed Mr. Whipple, and then acting on a sudden impulse added: 'Don't worry, my dear, it's only a temporary trouble. It will come all right, I think.'

She stared at him, her eyes wide.

'What do you mean?' she demanded. 'What do you know?'

'Quite a lot,' said Mr. Whipple, 'and I tell you not to worry.'

'I'm not worrying,' she said defiantly. 'I don't care tuppence — '

'Oh, yes, you do, my dear,' contradicted Mr. Whipple. 'You care many tuppences.'

Her lips parted to say something further and then, with a little choking sob, she turned and almost ran down the drive.

For the rest of that day, which was to end so dramatically, Mr. Whipple avoided the people at East Gables as much as possible. He had no desire to be questioned by Blanche Hislop, for he had nothing that he could reveal to her yet, and so he kept as much as possible out of the way. After lunch, when he had made sure he should not be overheard, he put through a cautious telephone call to Mr. Letten, and then when this was done, breathed a sigh of relief. His preparations were complete. It remained now to see what would come of them.

The evening brought an abrupt change in the weather. Heavy storm clouds began to bank up on the horizon and the sky became overcast. When Mr. Whipple left the house at half-past seven in order to walk into Godalming to keep his appointment with Inspector Gallers at the little police station, he took the precaution of providing himself with a light mackintosh. The atmosphere was so hot and strong that the walk was anything but enjoyable.

He arrived shortly before nine, limp, and exceedingly damp, to find that the two people he had asked to meet him had already arrived. Both Inspector Gallers and Mr. Letten were in the charge room talking to Blane.

'Good evening,' said Mr. Whipple as he

came in. 'It's really very good of you both. I hope that your trouble will be justified.'

He gratefully accepted the chair which Inspector Blane pushed forward and wiped his face.

'Have you — have you said anything to our friend here?'

Inspector Gallers shook his big head.

'No, Mr. Whipple,' he answered. 'I thought it was best to wait until you arrived.'

'That was extremely thoughtful of you,' said Mr. Whipple. 'Perhaps I had better then explain to Inspector Blane.'

'I think you had, sir,' said the inspector. 'I should very much like to know the reason for this conspiracy.'

Mr. Whipple began a little nervously, but his nervousness decreased as he proceeded. When he had finished Blane's face was a picture of astonishment.

'Well, gentlemen,' he said looking from one to the other. 'I must say you've taken my breath away. It sounds to me incredible.'

'I can't say that I'm completely

convinced,' said Inspector Gallers, 'but there can be no harm in trying Mr. Whipple's experiment, if you're agreeable, Inspector?'

'Oh, I'm agreeable,' said Blane. 'I'm open to conviction if Mr. Whipple can prove his case.'

'If this person turns up,' put in the lawyer quietly, 'it will go a very long way to proving his case.'

The local man nodded.

'I agree with that, sir,' he said.

'Then,' said Mr. Whipple, 'we'd better take up our positions in the summer-house at half-past twelve, and hope that we shall not be disappointed.'

★　★　★

The storm broke as they climbed into the police car, which Blane had ordered. The rain came down in torrents, the lightning and thunder were almost incessant. Mr. Whipple's unfortunate stomach went through a variety of convolutions as the car splashed its way towards Chittering.

It was five-and-twenty to one when, at

Mr. Whipple's direction, the driver brought the machine to a halt at the fringe of a small wood. They got out into the downpour and, led by Mr. Whipple, began to make their way slowly through the densely growing trees. During an exploration of the grounds of East Gables Mr. Whipple had discovered a small gate in the fence, which formed the borderline to the estate that opened directly on to this little wood. He reached it and waited while the others laboriously climbed the obstacle, for it was padlocked. When Inspector Gallers had helped him over they found themselves standing knee deep in undergrowth, beyond which lay a dense shrubbery.

The rain beat a continuous tattoo on the leaves above and around them, drowned every second or so by the crashing roar of the thunder overhead.

'Dear me, what a very unpleasant night!' gasped Mr. Whipple, as they forced their way through the dripping shrubbery and emerged onto a narrow winding path, almost ankle deep in water. 'This way, if you please.'

He followed the path that presently entered a broad walk of moss-grown flagstones, that ended in a small rustic summerhouse approached by a flight of three shallow steps. Towards this they made their way. The interior looked dark and forbidding, but they entered the little house with relief; for at least it was dry.

A bench ran along the entire back wall and on this they seated themselves and waited.

Around them hissed the rain and through the arched entrance as the lightning flickered, they could catch a glimpse of the long flagged path that bisected the rose garden and led to the big lawn at the back of East Gables. Along this path would come the person they awaited, the person whose clever brain had planned, and whose hand had carried out, the killing of Desmond Beal.

11

MR. WHIPPLE EXPLAINS

The vigil was not a long one, but their nerves were so keyed up with excitement that it seemed an age. The intense darkness of the little summerhouse, save when it was brilliantly lit by the reflected glare of the lightning; the monotonous hiss and splatter of the falling rain; the reverberating crashes of thunder, all combined to form an eerie setting to this last scene of the drama. In spite of all his efforts to control his emotions Mr. Whipple found himself trembling as though he were cold. He fully realized the tremendous responsibility that rested on his shoulders, for it had been he, and he alone, who had brought these people in the dead of night to keep watch for someone who might never arrive. If his carefully constructed theory was wrong then they would be wasting their time, for nothing would happen. If, on the other hand, he was right he failed to see what could prevent the murderer of Desmond Beal from putting in an appearance.

The minutes ticked slowly by. Mr. Whipple had an illuminated watch and on this he fixed his eye, watching the minute hand slowly move round towards the hour of one. Zero hour for all of them. It seemed to creep with infinite slowness, and more than once he held the little timepiece to his ear to make sure that it was still going.

By tacit consent they remained silent. Even if there had been anything to say the tense atmosphere would have prevented speech.

Slowly, incredibly slowly, the long hand moved until it was upright. One o'clock!

Mr. Whipple leaned forward, his eyes staring behind the lenses of his glasses, his breath coming irregularly between his slightly parted lips. Was the vigil to end in a fiasco or would the next few minutes prove him to have been right?

A peal of thunder drowned the gentle roar of the rain. It was followed a few seconds later by a blinding flash of blue-white light. Mr. Whipple heard the sharp hiss of indrawn breath beside him and caught his own, for in that instantaneous glare which lit up everything more brightly than the light of noon he had seen a figure enter the stone flagged path at the farther end.

Above the noise of the rain they could hear the sound of swiftly approaching footsteps, short, quick steps, and Mr. Whipple almost held his breath. A shadowy form loomed out of the darkness and drew near to the flight of steps leading up to the summerhouse. At the foot of them it paused, this figure in the long shining mackintosh and oil-skin hat, looked about, and mounting the three steps came through the arch into the darkness of the summerhouse.

'Now,' said Mr. Whipple, and would scarcely have recognized his own voice so hoarse and shaky was it.

A blinding ray of light leaped forward from the torch which Inspector Gallers had held ready for this moment, and focused itself on the newcomer. There was a sharp cry of alarm and the figure in the dripping mackintosh turned, but Inspector Blane had moved swiftly forward and was blocking the doorway. Like a trapped animal the figure in the mackintosh swung round again, its white face clearly visible in the brilliant ray of the torch, distorted with fear and fury, the face of Blanche Hislop.

'I — I think that proves my case,' said Mr. Whipple.

'I think it does, sir,' said Inspector Blane gravely, 'Would you mind explaining, Mrs. Hislop, what you are doing here at this time of night?'

Quickly, and to Mr. Whipple's reluctant admiration, the woman recovered herself. The distorting lines of hate and fear smoothed themselves from her face. Her big eyes opened wide and she looked from one to the other with an admirable assumption of bewilderment.

'Why, Mr. Whipple!' she said. 'Inspector Blane! I don't understand. Why shouldn't I be here? This is my property.'

'It seems peculiar, Madam,' said the inspector, 'that you should choose to visit it in the middle of the night and in a thunderstorm.'

'I couldn't sleep,' she began, but he interrupted her.

'Would you mind turning out your pockets?' he said, and at his words, sheer, naked terror flashed to her eyes.

'I should mind very much,' she said indignantly. 'By what right — '

But Inspector Blane was wasting no more time. With a swift movement he gripped her arm.

'Search her, will you?' he said sharply, and Gallers moved forward and dipped his hands quickly into the pockets of the mackintosh.

He withdrew a crumpled sheet of paper. Spreading it out he read the message in printed characters that Mr. Whipple had so laboriously penned on the Sunday night.

'*Your secret is known to me. It has not died with Beal. If you want to avoid trouble and fuss you had better meet me at one o'clock on Monday night in the summerhouse in your grounds.*'

There was no signature.

'That's conclusive, I think,' grunted Gallers, and broke off as Inspector Blane uttered a warning cry.

'Look out!' he exclaimed. 'She — '

But he was too late. With a sudden wrench Blanche Hislop had torn her right arm free of his grasp. Her hand flew to her breast and emerged clutching the butt of a tiny pistol. Before they could stop her there was a sharp report, and with a little half sigh, half groan, she crumpled up at their feet and lay still.

'Dear me, how very dreadful!' exclaimed Mr. Whipple in horror. 'I should keep that pistol if I were you, inspector. It's the weapon with which she killed Desmond Beal!'

* * *

Mr. Whipple, a gaudy dressing gown wrapped round his small figure, sat in the drawing room at East Gables sipping the hot coffee that an amazed and horror-stricken Droxford had prepared when he had been hastily aroused and briefly acquainted with the news of the tragedy.

Mr. Letten, as representing Robert Hislop, had taken charge, and with Inspector Blane and Gallers was awaiting Mr. Whipple's explanation as to how the murder had been committed.

'I congratulate you, sir,' said Inspector Blane, looking at the little man with added respect. 'Though I don't know how you managed it.'

'It was really — er — very simple,' said Mr. Whipple modestly. 'It, it was more or less by accident that I got the idea, you know. It was that red queen in Beal's hand that worried me. I told you at the time. And then, in the train going to Waterloo it suddenly occurred to me what it might mean. I remembered on the night when I first came down here that Mrs. Hislop was dressed in rather a vivid gown of scarlet and it occurred to me that — er — the red chess piece in Beal's hand had been a last moment effort on the part of the dead man — er — to give a clue to the person who had killed him. You understand?' He looked from one to the other. 'The red queen! Red, signifying the scarlet dress that Mrs. Hislop had worn, and queen, the sex of the murderer. At first of course — er — the whole idea — er — seemed to be ridiculous, because — er — at the time of the murder Mrs. Hislop was in the drawing room with Miss Wier, and unless — er — Miss Wier was an accomplice — er — it was impossible. At the same time — er — there seemed no harm in using it as a basis to try and form a — er — theory.

'I — I remembered the words I had overheard Miss Linden use to someone unknown, and coupling them with an expression I have seen in Geoffrey Ryman's — er — eyes when he looked at Mrs. Hislop I came to the conclusion that they were the utterances of a jealous woman, and that they had been addressed to Ryman. This was more or less confirmed when — when I learned that Mr. Ryman and Miss Linden had at one time been engaged. What she was telling him that night was — er — was that it was obvious he was in love with Blanche Hislop. 'Only a fool would think otherwise,' or something to that effect.

'It then occurred to me that perhaps he

was not only in love with Blanche Hislop but possibly Mrs. Hislop was in love with him, which meant, of course, that — er — her husband would be rather an obstacle. Supposing — er — she had decided to kill two birds with one stone, as it were. Get rid of Beal, who was blackmailing her, and by making it appear that Robert Hislop was guilty — er — get rid of him, too. I had read of a similar situation in — er — a book, called *Murder at the Abbey.*'

Mr. Whipple paused, took a sip of coffee and went on apologetically.

'At first, of course, it seemed very far fetched. I was presuming a great deal without any evidence to back it up. But allowing — er — for the fact that Beal had meant to try and signify who had killed him by grabbing the red queen as he died, it seemed — er — that it might be a possible explanation. And — er — the more I thought it over the more possible it became. There was another thing, too, which strengthened the motive. With Robert Hislop's death his wife would come into a large sum of money. He had told me once, during a conversation, that he had left everything to her, and I knew that the sum involved was something in the region of a quarter of a million. The great stumbling block was how had she managed to commit the murder while she was in the company of Miss Wier in another room? It then occurred to me that possibly the shot I had heard — er — the shot we all heard, was not the actual shot that killed Beal. And if this was the case then at the time he actually met his death Mrs. Hislop might not have been in the drawing room at all. But the revolver which was found lying beside the body, and which Robert picked up when he made the discovery had, evidently, been recently fired. And it was the report of that which everyone had undoubtedly heard.

'I remembered,' Mr. Whipple looked a trifle guilty, 'reading an incident whereby — er — a criminal had — er — faked an alibi by — by making the actual time of the crime seem later than it really was and appear to have taken place while the murderer was in the presence of someone else. This suggested to me that possibly something of the sort had occurred in this case. But there was — er — no — er — suggestion of a clock having been put on or back, or anything of that nature, and I couldn't conceive how a revolver could have been fired in one room while the person who — er — wished it to go off was in another.

'On my return from London, however, I witnessed a peculiar incident.' Mr. Whipple related what he had seen in the study. 'When I searched the room on the Sunday,' he continued, 'I found that someone had bored a small hole in the wainscoting near the fireplace right through into the drawing room. Mrs. Hislop had, of course, come down that night to plug the hole and so — er — hide up any traces of the method she had used to supply herself with an alibi. On the edges of the hole were some minute pieces of fluff, and I saw at once what had taken place. The whole thing had been very carefully planned.

'She had received the note from Beal stipulating the time limit, and had arranged, verbally, I suppose, to meet him in the study shortly before twelve-thirty. I've no doubt her plans had been laid long in advance, and she had merely been waiting an opportunity to carry them out. On the night before, she deliberately made some small adjustment to her clock so that it would stop at twelve-thirty, knowing from her husband's habits that if she told him it required repairing he would attend to it at twelve-thirty on the following day.

'That would ensure his being upstairs. She met Beal in the study at the appointed time, shot him with that small pistol which she used so tragically tonight, deadening the sound of the report by using a silencer. The moment he was dead — I don't think she noticed that he had picked up the red queen — she took Robert Hislop's revolver out of the drawer where he kept it, made sure it was loaded — she was, of course, wearing gloves so that — er — her fingerprints wouldn't be left — and through the hole from the drawing room which she had made in readiness, pulled a loop of string. Resting the revolver against the dead man's leg so that the barrel pointed towards the open French windows, she looped the string round the trigger and carried the two ends back through the hole. Then she went out and joined Miss Wier in the drawing room. When the time was ripe for the crime to be discovered all she had to do was to give a sharp jerk to both ends of the string and so explode the pistol.

'I had a word with Miss Wier, and she said at the time the shot was fired Mrs. Hislop was bending down by the fireplace in the drawing room tying her shoe lace. Under cover of this she was able to give the required jerk to the string, and at the same time to pull on one end of it, which, of course, left the other end slack and so she was able to retrieve the string through the hole, leaving no sign of the mechanism by which she had succeeded in — er — establishing her alibi.

'It was, of course, because the bullet had passed through nothing to offer it an obstruction — er — that it couldn't be found. You see it — it had possibly travelled in a slight arc and gone much further than one would expect if it had first gone through the head of the dead man.

'All she had to do after this, at her leisure, was to place the note which Beal had written to her in Robert Hislop's dressing gown pocket, and the evidence against him was complete. It was sheer luck, of course, that made him the first person to discover the body, and it wasn't necessary to her scheme. The fact that only his fingerprints were on the revolver that had apparently killed the man and the note in his dressing gown pocket were quite sufficient. Once you were on the right track it — er — was, of course, really very simple. The great difficulty was to prove it. Here I'm afraid' — Mr. Whipple shook his head — 'it was my fondness for reading thrilling fiction that helped me again.

'I remembered a story called the *Five Dead Goldfish* in which the detective faced with a similar situation to my own, had set a trap for the murderer. I — er — wrote the note to Mrs. Hislop to give her the impression of someone else besides Beal knowing her secret, the secret for which he had blackmailed her, and she — er — fell into the trap, as I hoped and expected she would. Well, that's all, I think,' he ended with relief, and finished his coffee.

'I wonder what this secret was that Beal was holding over her?' muttered Letten, but nobody was able to tell him for nobody knew.

And they did not find out until nearly a fortnight later when the police investigations revealed the fact that at the time Blanche Edington had married Robert Hislop she had been already married to Desmond Beal.

'It was just as well, I think, Mr. Whipple,' said Inspector Gallers, one evening as he and his next door neighbour conversed over the intervening fence, 'that she committed suicide that night. It would have all been very painful for your friend.'

Mr. Whipple agreed.

'Yes, I think so, too,' he said, and wondered, as he had wondered many times since, whether Robert Hislop had been suspicious of his wife from the beginning. That air of watchful vigilance that he had surmised. Was it because he had seen through Geoffrey Ryman's obvious infatuation, or was it because he was suspicious of Beal.

Mr. Whipple remembered the revolver cleaning incident in the middle of the night, and was inclined to believe that Hislop had suspected intrigue between Ryman and his wife.

'Though I must say,' said Inspector Gallers, nipping a greenfly off one of his roses, 'that you worked the whole thing out very cleverly, Mr. Whipple.'

Mr. Whipple blushed. 'I don't — er — think,' he stammered nervously, 'that it was — er — entirely — that the credit should go — er — to me, altogether. It was remembering incidents in the various books I had read that — er — more or less put me on the right track.'

'I suppose so,' said Inspector Gallers thoughtfully. 'Yes, there must be something useful about these detective stories after all.

RED SNOW

1

THE GAME

The snow, which was destined to play such a large part in the tragic happenings of that weekend, began to fall at nine-fifteen on the Friday. The day had been a cold one, bright in the morning but clouding over in the afternoon with those smooth, grey, leaden clouds that nearly always herald the approach of snow.

Mr. Augustus Whipple diffidently remarked on this to his host, Colonel Shand, the Chief Constable for Blankshire, as they walked back across the Horne Park for luncheon.

Mr. Whipple had been friendly with Shand for years although as a rule they saw very little of each other. The little draper had first been introduced to the Chief Constable by his friend, Inspector Gallers, during one of the Colonel's infrequent visits to Scotland Yard on business. Shand had taken a liking to the shy little man, and since they both possessed a common love of detective fiction they became friends, though this was the first time Shand had succeeded in persuading Mr. Whipple to pay a long-promised visit to Longford Chase.

An old gabled house of the Tudor period, it stood on the outskirts of the little village of Great Lindreck in three and a half acres of wooded ground. At one time it had been the Manor House, but it had been empty for nearly five years when the Colonel had bought it. He had spent a great deal of money in repairs, and taken a lot of care in filling the house with genuine antiques and furniture which matched the stone walls, oak panelling and massive beams. With its wide brick fireplaces in which the sweet scented pine-logs burnt merrily, its leaded windows and tiled floors it was a house of peace and beauty that delighted Mr. Whipple's heart.

Shand was a widower, his wife had died in India from the effects of a mosquito

bite which had turned to blood poison-
ing, and although this had happened
fifteen years previously the Colonel had
never quite got over his loss; there was
just a touch of sadness to be seen now
and again in his grey eyes, and in the set
of his mouth. The whole interest of his
life was centred on his son, a good-
looking boy of twenty-one, to whom Mr.
Whipple had taken an instant liking.

'I've got a man coming down this
evening,' said Shand as they strode along,
'whom I think you'll be interested to
meet.'

'Yes?' said Mr. Whipple a little breathlessly, for he found it difficult to keep up
with his long-legged companion.

'I expect you know him quite well by
reputation,' went on the Colonel, 'John
Ramsden.'

'Do you mean the — the thriller
writer?' said Mr. Whipple in a hushed
voice.

'That's the fellow,' replied his host. 'I
suppose you've read his stories?'

The little man nodded.

'Yes,' he replied. 'All of them.'

'So have I,' said Shand. 'I think they're jolly good.'

'They're certainly very ingenious,' said Mr. Whipple. 'I didn't know he was a friend of yours.'

'As a matter of fact he isn't a friend of mine,' answered the Colonel. 'He's a friend of Dick's. The boy met him at a cocktail party in town, I believe, and saw quite a lot of him afterwards. He persuaded me to invite him and his wife down for the weekend.'

'I shall be most interested to meet him,' said Mr. Whipple. 'Are you — are you having a large party?'

Shand shook his head.

'No,' he answered. 'Including ourselves, about a dozen. I think it will be quite a pleasant crowd.'

Mr. Whipple hoped so. His nervous nature made him dislike meeting fresh people.

'I don't think you know any of them,' continued the Colonel. 'Unless it's Jackson, you might know him. He used to be an inspector at the Yard, but he's been retired now on a pension for about three years. He lives in a cottage in the village; quite a nice fellow. I asked him because he was going to be all on his own and some of his reminiscences are interesting.'

'I — I don't think I know him,' replied Mr. Whipple. 'Probably Inspector Gallers does.'

Gallers was coming down later that day, to Mr. Whipple's relief. At least his would be a familiar one among the strange faces he had to meet.

They began talking about other things and reached the house just as the gong was sounding for lunch.

The first of the expected guests arrived just after four, a man who was introduced to Mr. Whipple as Captain Egerton. He was small and rather dapper, with a tiny wisp of moustache, and he stared very hard at the little man until he felt himself redden with embarrassment. The arrival of Egerton seemed to have broken the ice, for shortly afterward the rest of the guests began to arrive in ones and twos.

There were two girls who Mr. Whipple gathered were sisters, and whose name sounded like Weston. He wasn't quite sure of this because he hadn't been able to hear it properly. There was a middle-aged, dark-haired man, rather stout, called Mortimer, whose face Mr. Whipple thought was familiar, although he couldn't for the life of him remember where he had seen the man before. The retired inspector, Jackson, put in an appearance coincidently with Gallers, whom he had apparently met on the way from the station. The last to arrive was Ramsden, with his wife. He was a fat, chubby-faced man with grey hair and many chins, and his voice was very loud and booming. He radiated an air of cheerfulness and good humour and was, Mr. Whipple decided, a very likeable fellow indeed. Mrs. Ramsden was much younger than her husband, small and slim, with rather pretty fair hair that clung in curls to her shapely head.

'How do you do, Mr. Whipple?' boomed John Ramsden when he was first introduced. 'I've been looking forward to meeting you.'

'Dear me, that's very nice of you,' said Mr. Whipple uneasily. 'I — I sincerely hope you're not going to be disappointed.'

The other chuckled. He did this very readily, and on all conceivable occasions. It was not so much a sign of amusement as a nervous mannerism.

'I read of your connection with that business at Chittering a few months ago,' he said, 'and I thought the way you worked it out was ingenious.'

Mr. Whipple stuttered something incoherently and slunk away into a corner, wishing devoutly that he had never left his small neat house at Balham.

It was during dinner that night that the first seed of the tragedy that was to come was sown. It started from one of those apparently innocent remarks which, innocuous in themselves, so often have far-reaching results

The conversation had drifted through various easy stages from art to literature; and from books in general to John Ramsden's in particular was but a step. Shand had just told the complacent author how much he had enjoyed his latest novel when Egerton made the remark, which turned out to be the lighted match applied to the fuse.

'I enjoyed that book, too,' he said: 'Tell me, Mr. Ramsden, why do you always make your detective an amateur? Why don't you let the official police solve the crime? Surely it would be more true to life?'

John Ramsden gave vent to one of his particularly fruity chuckles.

'I do it because my public likes it,' he replied, 'and I'm not so sure that it isn't true to life after all.' He looked across to Mr. Whipple and his eyes twinkled. 'You can prove that, can't you?' he said. 'You succeeded in that Hislop business when the police had failed.'

Mr. Whipple squirmed uneasily in his chair. It was a particularly embarrassing moment, he thought. With Inspector Gallers representing Scotland Yard and the Official Police Force sitting almost immediately opposite him he felt rather at a loss what to say.

'I — I was certainly very lucky,' he mumbled at length.

'There's no such thing as luck,' grunted

Mr. Mortimer. 'The man who is considered lucky is usually a little more efficient than his fellows, that's all.'

'Might I suggest,' said Egerton, twisting the stem of his wineglass delicately between his fingers, 'that probably the reason Mr. Whipple was successful was because he made greater use of his imagination.'

'I agree with that,' John Ramsden nodded quickly. 'I think that's what the police lack.'

Inspector Gallers, who, up to now had been listening in silence, shook his head.

'Imagination's all very well in its place,' he said slowly, 'but police work in real life isn't the same as in stories, Mr. Ramsden. We are not introduced to all the characters at the beginning and asked to pick out the guilty one. We don't know any of 'em. All we've got in a murder case is the dead man. Sometimes we don't even know who he is, what he is, his private business, his relations, or anything about him. We've got to find all that out. That doesn't mean imagination — only hard work.'

'That's quite right, Gallers,' said ex-Inspector Jackson. 'Routine and endless questions, that's police work. Ceaseless enquiries here, there, and everywhere.'

'That's probably all right for ninety-nine cases out of a hundred,' argued the author, 'but what about the hundredth? I'll back the man with imagination every time against the man who works purely by routine.'

'I think you'd lose, Ramsden,' put in Colonel Shand quietly. 'The police are not such fools as you writers make out.'

'I'm not saying they're fools!' protested Ramsden. 'With the sort of crime they come up against they're perfectly all right, but give them a problem to work on — the kind of murder mysteries that I write for instance — and I maintain that they'd be absolutely baffled.'

It was at this point in the conversation that Egerton made his fatal suggestion.

'Why not murder somebody and see?' he remarked, and then, as everybody at the table stared at him: 'Oh, I don't mean really, of course. I mean let Ramsden supply a plot, complete with clues, and let Mr. Whipple and Detective-Inspector Gallers start off equally and see which of them solves the problem first.'

'By jove, Egerton,' exclaimed Dick Shand, 'that's a great idea! You mean the murder game with variations?'

'Exactly!' replied Egerton, a glint of amusement in his eyes. 'It ought to be amusing.'

The idea was hailed with delight by everybody, specially the two Miss Westons. The only people who did not seem particularly enthusiastic were Gallers, Mr. Whipple, and Mr. Mortimer. As a matter of fact Mr. Whipple was feeling extremely uncomfortable. The thought of being dragged into the limelight produced a peculiar sensation in the pit of his stomach, which he always associated with thunderstorms, and which was anything but pleasant. He could see by the expression on Gallers' face, too, that he was none too pleased. He felt, however, that it would be churlish to refuse, and so he contented himself with saying nothing.

John Ramsden was openly as pleased as a child with a new toy.

'It 'ud be great fun,' he boomed. 'We'll toss up who's to be the corpse and then I'll think out the story.'

'I tell you what,' said Dick, 'we'll draw lots. Leaving out Mr. Whipple and Inspector Gallers there are nine of us. I'll put nine slips of paper into a hat on one of which I'll write 'body'; whoever draws that will have to be the 'corpse.''

'That's good,' said Ramsden, grinning. 'But you'd better let me out because I've got to plan the thing.'

'That makes eight.' Dick pushed back his chair and rose to his feet. 'I'll get some paper.'

'Let's finish dinner first,' protested Shand.

'It won't take a minute, Dad,' said Dick, 'and it'll give Mr. Ramsden longer to think out his plot once we've decided who's going to be killed.'

He hurried out of the room and was back again in a few seconds with a sheet of notepaper and a hat which he had taken off the stand in the hall.

'Here we are,' he said, reseating himself, and began to divide the sheet of paper into eight slips. On one of these he wrote the word 'body', put the whole lot into the hat and gave it a shake. 'Now then, let's see who's going to die,' he said with a grin. 'I'll have the first pick.'

He held the hat high in the air, put his hand into it, and took out one of the pieces of paper. After a hasty glance at it he dropped it onto his plate.

'Not me,' he said. 'You're next, Egerton.'

He passed the hat along to Egerton who drew from it, looked at the result and shook his head, passing the hat along to Mortimer. Rather reluctantly that gentleman thrust in his hand and withdrew his slip of paper. He darted a look at it and then glanced round the ring of faces a little startled.

'You needn't trouble to go any farther,' he said in a low, strained voice. 'I'm the body!'

'It couldn't have been anybody better,' chuckled John Ramsden. 'If you don't mind my saying so you'll make an excellent corpse!' He broke into a booming laugh, stretched out his hand, took a nut and cracked it. 'You'd better give me until tomorrow,' he went on, 'to think the whole thing out in detail. What time are we breakfasting, Shand?'

'When you like,' answered the Chief Constable. 'I'll be ready from eight-thirty onwards.'

'Well, I suggest,' said Ramsden, 'that all of us, with the exception, of course, of Whipple and Gallers, meet here at nine-thirty, and I'll have the whole thing cut and dried.'

This was agreed upon, and except for some chaffing remarks to Mortimer the subject was dropped.

Mr. Whipple thought about it, however, a good deal during the rest of the evening, and it recurred to him again as he was undressing to go to bed. For some inexplicable reason he felt uneasy, filled with a sense of foreboding that he couldn't shake off. Just before he got into bed he went to the window and looked out. It was snowing heavily.

2

THE REALITY

Mr. Whipple awoke in the morning with a vague feeling that something was wrong. He had slept remarkably well and had not wakened until he had been aroused by the maid bringing him morning tea, and as he sipped the hot fluid he tried to account for his peculiar sensation. And then he remembered the conversation at the dinner table on the previous night. That was it, of course! This absurd suggestion of Egerton's. Today he and Gallers were supposed to attempt to solve some ridiculous problem of Ramsden's.

He frowned a little irritably as he got up and searched for his dressing gown. He was not looking forward to it in the least, in fact he heartily disliked the whole idea. He had no wish whatever to pit himself against the inspector in this childish competition.

With his usual meticulous care he bathed, shaved and dressed and made his way downstairs. It was twenty minutes past eight when he entered the dining room, and apparently he was the first of the party up, for the room was empty.

Going over to the window he peered out at the mantle of white that covered the landscape. The snow was still falling, but not so heavily as it had been, and turning to the fireplace he picked up *The Times* and began to skim through the pages. He had just finished the leading article when Colonel Shand came in.

''Morning, Whipple,' he greeted. 'By jove, it's cold!'

'I should say it was freezing hard,' said Mr. Whipple. 'The snow looks like stopping.'

'There can't be much more of it to come,' said the Colonel. 'How did you sleep — all right?'

'Excellently, thank you,' replied Mr. Whipple.

'Good!' said his host, warming his hands by the fire. 'Then you'll be in form for this business of Ramsden's.'

'I — I yes, I suppose so,' said Mr. Whipple uneasily, and Shand shot him a sidelong glance.

'You don't seem very enthusiastic,' he remarked.

'Really — er — er — to be quite candid, I — I'm not!' said Mr. Whipple. 'I don't really — relish the idea at all.'

'If you feel like that about it,' said the Colonel, 'I'll call it off.'

'Dear me, no, no don't do that,' said Mr. Whipple quickly, horrified at the thought that he should be the one to spoil anybody's enjoyment. 'The others are — er — looking forward to it, I don't doubt, and I wouldn't like to disappoint them.'

'I am, I must say,' said the Chief Constable. 'I think it's going to be rather exciting.'

Ramsden came in at that moment looking the picture of health. He greeted them with a cheery 'good morning' and almost immediately plunged into the matter of the mock murder.

'I've thought it all out,' he said. 'Didn't go to bed until after four — Mildred was cursing like Hell — and I've got a real snorter of a problem!' He turned to Mr. Whipple and beamed. 'I'll bet you've never come up against anything like it.'

His enthusiasm was so evident that the little man felt it would be unkind not to force some show of interest.

'I assure you, Mr. Ramsden,' he said, 'that I will do my best to solve your riddle. When are we supposed to start?'

'As soon as we've had breakfast I'll explain the whole thing,' said Ramsden. 'Of course you and Gallers will have to clear out while we set the scene of the crime.'

'As far as I can see,' said Shand smiling, 'Mortimer's going to have the best time. He starts off by being dead and remains dead all day, whereas we shall have to spend our time answering questions and proving alibis and whatnot.'

'Mostly whatnot,' said Dick, entering at that moment with Jackson. 'Good morning, everybody.'

He was followed almost immediately by the butler with coffee and several covered dishes that gave forth an appetizing smell.

'Food!' he cried. 'I don't know about anybody else, but I'm ravenous. This cold weather always makes me hungry. He grabbed a plate and went over to the sideboard and examined the contents of the dishes as Hollick, the butler, removed them from the wagon. 'Come on, those who want breakfast. There's eggs and bacon, grilled kidneys, sausages and kedgeree,' he said. 'You pays your penny and takes your choice.'

'What d'you get for tuppence?' enquired the cool voice of Egerton from the doorway.

'Double quantity,' grinned Dick. He helped himself to some bacon and grilled kidneys and went over to the table.

'Well,' said Egerton, 'how's the murder going?'

Ramsden looked round from the sideboard with a grin.

'Fine!' he said. 'Everything's planned to the last detail.'

'The 'body' isn't down yet I see,' said Jackson.

'The meeting was arranged for nine-thirty,' said the novelist, 'and it's only just nine.'

As though in confirmation of his words the clock in the hall softly chimed the hour. Claire Weston, the prettiest of the two sisters, put in an appearance a few minutes later. Lucy, she informed them, wasn't feeling very well and was having her breakfast in bed.

'So's my wife,' said Ramsden, 'but that's my fault for keeping her awake half the night.'

'Why did you do that?' asked the girl in surprise.

'He was planning how to murder Mortimer,' said Dick. 'Crime takes a lot of thinking out.'

'Have you succeeded?' asked Claire, smiling at Ramsden.

The novelist nodded with his mouth full of sausage.

'I have,' he mumbled. 'I've planned the perfect crime.'

'We shall see how long it takes the experts to discover your murderer,' said Egerton, and there was the hint of a sneer in his voice.

'Who is going to be the murderer, Mr. Ramsden?' asked the girl.

'You'll know that at nine-thirty,' he replied, 'Until then I'm as dumb as an oyster.'

They began to talk about general subjects and the clock was just striking nine-thirty when Mr. Whipple got up from the table and moved over to the door.

'I suppose I had better leave you now,' he said, 'to — er — to carry on your murderous intentions without interruptions.' He smiled. 'What time are you likely to be finished?'

'I think about half an hour should see us through,' answered Ramsden. 'We'll give you a call.'

'If you see Gallers,' said Shand, 'tell him I'll have his breakfast sent into the library.'

Mr. Whipple nodded, and he was in the act of leaving the room — in fact he had the door half-open in his hand — when from somewhere in the house came a loud report. The party at the breakfast table heard it and looked up, startled.

'What the devil was that — ' began the Chief Constable, half-rising from his chair, but before he could say anything more they heard Gallers calling frantically from somewhere above.

'Colonel Shand!' he cried. 'Come here quickly, will you?'

Before the Colonel could move, Mr. Whipple was across the hall and halfway up the stairs.

'Where — where are you?' he quavered.

'Is that you, Mr. Whipple?' said Gallers. 'I'm here, in Mortimer's room.'

Mr. Whipple reached the landing and hurried along the corridor. Halfway down he saw Gallers standing looking through the open door of a room on the left. The air was full of a pungent, acrid smell, like hot iron, and as he reached the inspector's side Gallers turned, his usually florid face grey.

'What — what is the matter?' stammered Mr. Whipple.

'Look for yourself!' muttered Gallers, and pointed through the open door into the room beyond.

Mr. Whipple looked and caught his breath.

The window was open and lying half

across the sill, so that his head and shoulders were outside, was the figure of a man. Mr. Whipple crossed the room quickly and peered into the upturned face. It was James Mortimer, and he was dead — killed by the bullet that had made such a neat hole in the centre of his forehead.

3

RED SNOW

The sound of footsteps and excited voices warned Mr. Whipple that the others were coming up the stairs to investigate the cause of the disturbance. Turning hastily, and rather thankfully, away from the dead man by the window, he went over to the door, and slipping out, closed it gently behind him.

Colonel Shand, followed by Dick and Ramsden, appeared at the end of the corridor, and Mr. Whipple went nervously to meet them.

'What's the matter?' asked Shand quickly, as he saw the serious expression on the little man's face.

'I'm afraid there's been rather an unfortunate accident, Colonel,' said Mr. Whipple. 'Mr. — er — Mortimer — er — is dead!'

'Dead? Good God!' Ramsden's round,

chubby face was horrified. 'How did it happen?'

'He has been shot!' replied Mr. Whipple in a hushed voice.

'Suicide?' whispered Colonel Shand, and Mr. Whipple shook his head.

'I don't think so,' he answered, with a worried look. 'No, I'm very much afraid it's — it wasn't suicide. Don't you — don't you think it would be a good idea to keep everybody downstairs?'

'Yes, certainly!' said the Colonel, and he turned to the head of the stairs.

Mr. Whipple looked at Gallers.

'If,' he said hesitantly, 'you wouldn't mind telling me exactly how you made the discovery?'

'I was just coming along the corridor,' answered the Scotland Yard man, 'when I heard the sound of a shot. I tried the door, found it was unlocked, opened it and saw him exactly as he is now.' He jerked his head towards the body sprawled across the sill.

'You were in sight of the door when you heard the shot?' asked the little man, perplexedly, and Gallers nodded.

'Dear me,' said Mr. Whipple, frowning, and rubbing his chin. 'Then it would seem to be impossible for anyone to have left the room without you seeing them?'

'Quite impossible!' declared the inspector. 'I was barely two yards from the door when the shot was fired. It must have been suicide!'

'It certainly appears like it,' admitted Mr. Whipple reluctantly. 'But I can't see any sign of the weapon.'

'Probably it fell out of the window,' suggested Gallers. 'From the position of the body it looks to me as if he must have been standing by the open window when he shot himself.'

'That's very possible,' agreed Mr. Whipple. 'Yes, very possible indeed.' He moved over and carefully noted the position of the dead man. 'He's fallen backwards across the sill, as you see,' he remarked presently, 'which seems to show that he was facing towards the door when he died.'

'Unless,' said the inspector, 'the shock of the bullet's impact caused him to twist round, throwing the revolver out of the window as he did so. As there is no sign of the weapon in the room, that's what must have happened.'

'No doubt if that is the case we shall find it somewhere down below,' said Mr. Whipple, but he appeared entirely unconvinced. 'We'll finish up here and then go down, shall we?'

Taking care not to disturb the body, he leaned out of the window and peered down. The expanse of virgin snow was unbroken, and although he looked carefully he could see no marks that might have been made by the weapon. Withdrawing his head he began a closer inspection of the body than he, had done heretofore, and almost at once he found something, which caused his face to wrinkle perplexedly.

The wound on the forehead was small, but at the back of the head was a larger one where the bullet had made its exit, and the hair around this was matted with blood that had already frozen solid. It was not this second wound which brought that peculiar expression to the little man's face, it was the fact that there were no powder-marks on the dead man's forehead.

'I'm very much afraid this is not suicide after all,' he said nervously, and pointed out his discovery to Gallers. 'I'm sure you will agree with me that you can't fire a shot at close quarters without leaving marks.'

Gallers walked over and glared down at the motionless figure.

'You're right, Mr. Whipple,' he muttered. 'But how the deuce could it have happened? He couldn't have been shot from outside. The shot was fired from inside this room — I'll swear to that!'

'I am prepared to agree with you,' said Mr. Whipple. 'We heard the report downstairs, and I smelt the — the burnt powder in the corridor. But if that is the case, who fired it and how did they get away?'

'Can anybody have escaped by the window?' suggested Gallers.

They went together and examined the sill. It was covered by two inches of snow, which, except where the body had fallen had not been disturbed.

'No, there's no sign of anybody having got out this way,' grunted the inspector. It would have been impossible for them to have done so without leaving traces.'

'Unless the murderer had the power to make himself invisible,' remarked Mr. Whipple, 'he couldn't have got out by the door.'

'So the whole thing's impossible,' growled Gallers.

'It appears to be so on the face of it,' said the little draper. 'But there must be some explanation. Mortimer is obviously — er — dead, and the shot that killed him must have been fired by somebody.'

He stopped abruptly and stared at the dead man's right hand, which was tightly clenched.

Through the interstices of the fingers he had caught a faint glimpse of something black. Gently he prised open that stiff grasp and a small object fell out into the palm of his hand. It was a lump of coal!

Mr. Whipple looked at it, completely bewildered. How on earth had it got into the dead man's hand? He turned towards the fireplace, but there was no coal there. As in his own bedroom, the grate had been fitted with a gas fire. How, then, had this come into Mortimer's possession? He looked at the little black lump carefully, turning it this way and that in his fingers, while Gallers watched him, his face expressive of his amazement. It was a very ordinary piece of coal, about the size of a large walnut, and Mr. Whipple could think of no reasonable explanation for its presence.

'Another mystery,' muttered the inspector, rubbing the back of his neck. 'What the devil was he doing with it, and how did it get there?'

Mr. Whipple shook his head.

'Really, I haven't the least idea,' he replied. 'From the way his fingers were — er — gripped round it, it must have been in his hand, I should think, when he died.' He wrapped it in his handkerchief and absent-mindedly dropped it into his pocket. 'Did you — did you hear anything before the sound of the shot?' he enquired, and Gallers shook his head.

'No, nothing!' he answered.

Mr. Whipple looked at him curiously, and rather diffidently put the question that had been worrying him.

'What — what were you doing in this corridor at all?' he said. 'Your room is on the next floor, isn't it?'

'Yes.' The Scotland Yard man looked a little embarrassed, and there was a perceptible pause before he continued. 'As a matter of fact,' he said, slowly at last, 'I was coming to see Mortimer.'

'Dear me,' said Mr. Whipple in astonishment. 'Why?'

'Because he asked me to,' replied Gallers. He searched in his pocket and took out an envelope. Thrusting his fingers into it he drew out a single sheet of paper and held it out to the little man. 'Read that,' he said.

Mr. Whipple took it and peered through his glasses at the lines of sprawling writing.

Will you come and see me at nine-thirty? The matter is urgent and I want to discuss it with you before you see any of the others. I will wait in my room.

James Mortimer.

'Dear me, this is very interesting,' murmured Mr. Whipple. 'How did you get it?'

'I found it pushed under my door when I woke this morning,' answered Gallers.

Mr. Whipple read the note through again, and his lips pursed.

'Might I — might I see the envelope?' he asked.

Gallers gave it him, and he saw that it was blank.

'It seems rather peculiar, don't you think,' he remarked, 'that he didn't address it?'

'I thought that,' said Gallers, 'but I concluded that he had been in a hurry and forgotten. He was obviously in a hurry when he wrote the note, you can tell that by the writing.'

Mr. Whipple's head moved up and down in a curious, bird-like manner.

'I suppose you've no idea why he was so anxious to see you?' he enquired.

'No,' answered Gallers. 'I was rather surprised when I got the note.'

'You — you didn't know Mortimer?' said Mr. Whipple. 'I mean, before you came down here?'

The Scotland Yard man shook his head.

'Never saw him before in my life!' he asserted.

Mr. Whipple wrinkled his sandy brows and stared at the letter, which he still held in his hand.

'I wonder what it was he wanted to see you about?' ' he murmured. 'From the wording of this note it looks as though he wanted to discuss something with you in your official capacity.'

'The thing that beats me,' said Gallers, 'is not why, but how? The man has been shot, but nobody was in the room. They couldn't have been.'

'And with the exception of the servants, Mrs. Ramsden, Lucy Weston, and yourself,' put in Mr. Whipple, 'the rest of the people in the house have got excellent alibis, for at the time the shot was fired they were all in the dining room.'

Gallers smiled, a little queerly.

'Well, this is a bigger puzzle for us to solve than Ramsden could have thought out,' he grunted. 'By gosh, it's strange, Mr. Whipple, that Mortimer was chosen to act the part of the 'corpse' and then this happening!'

'Most strange,' agreed the little man. 'Er — do you think we — we might have a look through Mortimer's effects? We might find something that would help us.'

There were two suitcases standing by the foot of the bed, but both of these had been unpacked and were empty. A glance at the wardrobe disclosed a lounge suit and the dress suit the dead man had worn on the previous night, both neatly put away on hangers. They went carefully through the pockets, but they found nothing. A dressing gown, lying across the bottom of the bed, next occupied their attention, but again they drew a blank. Neither was there anything of importance in the drawers of the dressing table or on the dressing chest.

The bedroom, like all the others, was provided with a small writing table, and here Mr. Whipple made a discovery. In the waste paper basket he found a crumpled up piece of notepaper which, when it was spread out, proved to be the beginning of a letter. There were only two lines of writing, but it was obviously Mortimer's for it was the same, sprawling hand as the note that he had sent to Gallers.

I am not going to submit to this persecution any longer. Your superiors —
ors —

That was all — the writing ended abruptly.

Apparently Mortimer had changed his mind about the wording or decided not to write the letter at all.

'This,' said Mr. Whipple, showing it to Gallers, 'looks as if — er — blackmail might be at the bottom of this business. I wonder what he means by 'superiors', and who this letter was intended for?'

'One of the servants perhaps,' suggested the inspector. 'That would account for the words 'your superiors'.'

163

'Yes, maybe,' answered Mr. Whipple, but his voice was a little doubtful. 'It doesn't seem quite the right phrase, to me.' He peered short-sightedly round the room. 'I suppose we'd better not touch the — the body,' he said, 'until after the police and the doctor have seen it?'

'No,' said Gallers, 'we'll lock the door and have a look round outside.'

They left the room, with its silent occupant, and, locking the door, Gallers put the key in his pocket. In the hall downstairs they found Colonel Shand, his face grave and troubled.

'I've telephoned the police,' he said, 'and they're on their way now. What a dreadful thing to have happened? I wonder why he did it?'

'He — er — he didn't do it,' said Mr. Whipple gently.

The Colonel stared at him, and his troubled expression changed to a look of surprise.

'You don't mean,' he whispered, almost inaudibly, 'that it wasn't suicide?'

Mr. Whipple nodded.

'I'm afraid I do,' he answered, as

though it was entirely his fault. 'It was — er — murder! There's no doubt about it!'

'But how — ' began Shand, and Gallers interrupted him.

'We don't know how, or why, or what for, he declared. 'All we know at present is that a little after half-past nine this morning somebody shot James Mortimer. We are going outside now,' he went on, before Shand could reply. 'I think, Colonel, you'd better break the news to the rest of the household and see that nobody leaves until after the police have been.'

'I'll do that now,' said the Chief Constable, and hurried away.

They descended the snow-covered steps and made their way round to the side of the house where the window of Mortimer's room was situated. The snow had ceased, and it was not quite so cold as it had been. There was no difficulty in finding the place they sought, for the dead man's head and shoulders were plainly visible protruding from the open window. As they drew near Mr. Whipple suddenly stopped with a little gasp and clutched at his companion's arm.

'Dear me, look at that!' he murmured in astonishment.

Immediately beneath the window of the fatal room the snow, which had been entirely unsullied when he had looked from the window a few minutes before, had turned red; an irregular patch of scarlet that showed up, with startling distinctness, against the surrounding whiteness.

4

SUSPICION

'I don't see anything to be surprised about,' grunted Gallers, as he looked. 'It's blood.'

'Yes, yes, of course, it's blood,' said Mr. Whipple. 'But perhaps you could suggest — er — how it got there?'

His friend looked at him as though he had suddenly gone mad.

'What are you getting at?' he growled. 'Of course I can tell you how it got there. It came from the wound in Mortimer's head.'

'Did it?' said Mr. Whipple. 'But that's really most extraordinary.'

'Why is it extraordinary?' demanded the inspector.

'Because,' explained the little man, 'the wound had bled certainly, but it wasn't bleeding when I examined it. It had ceased to bleed, and the intense cold had

167

frozen what blood there was — and there was no mark then on the snow.'

Gallers bent forward and peered down at the sinister stain by the wall.

'Well, this is blood,' he answered. 'There's no doubt about that!'

Mr. Whipple stooped, suppressing a shudder, touched the patch with his finger and looked at the tip. It glistened redly.

'No, there's no doubt about it being blood,' he murmured, and the expression on his face was puzzled.

'If you look at the side of the house you'll see several splashes on the stone,' said Gallers, pointing them out as he spoke. 'That proves it's Mortimer's blood. You must have missed this patch when you looked out before.'

Mr. Whipple made no reply, but continued to stare at the red patch, his fingers nervously caressing his chin. He was perfectly certain he had not made a mistake. There had been *no* stain when he had looked down from the window of Mortimer's bedroom, and since the wound then had ceased to bleed it was rather curious how it had got there. He couldn't have missed it because he had been particularly looking for possible marks made by the dropped weapon and the snow then had been smooth, white, and unblemished.

He refrained from arguing with Gallers, however, and after making a careful search in the vicinity for any other traces, and finding none, they both returned to the house. As they came round the corner of the building they saw a car drawn up in front of the steps leading to the porch. Evidently the police had arrived during their absence.

In the hall they found Shand talking to a thin dark man, and a uniformed constable. Shand called Gallers as he came in and introduced the dark man as Inspector Pepper.

'We've been waiting for you,' said the inspector, in rather a surly voice. 'You've got the key of the room.'

'Sorry,' said Gallers. 'I'd no idea you'd arrived. Shall we go upstairs now?'

Inspector Pepper looked at the Chief Constable. It was obvious that he resented the Yard man's interference. Shand, seeing this, hastily tried to smooth things over.

'I think, since Inspector Gallers was present at the discovery,' he said, 'it would be as well if you continued your investigations together.'

Inspector Pepper looked anything but pleased, in fact he looked distinctly annoyed.

'That is for you to say, sir, of course,' he answered stiffly. 'I'm quite capable of attending to this business on my own.'

'I'm not suggesting that you're not, Inspector,' said the Colonel quickly. 'But since Inspector Gallers is here I think we ought to take advantage of his advice.'

'As you please, sir,' said Pepper. 'Are you ready, Doctor?' He called across to a man who had been standing examining a picture, a man of medium height with an almost completely bald head. What little hair he possessed grew in a fringe from his ears round the nape of his neck. He turned at the sound of the inspector's voice and nodded.

'Quite ready,' he said, coming over and

joining the group.

Shand introduced Mr. Whipple as they went upstairs. Reaching the door of the fatal room, Gallers took the key from his pocket and unlocked it.

'I'd better give this to you now,' he said, and Pepper took it with a grunt and thrust it into his pocket.

The Divisional Surgeon's examination was brief.

'Not much doubt how he died,' he said. 'The bullet passed through his brain and came out at the base of the skull. He must have died instantly.'

'Would — would there have been much blood?' enquired Mr. Whipple.

The doctor stared at him.

'Quite a quantity, in the ordinary course of events,' he answered. 'It looks to me as if the wound had been partially frozen, and that, of course, would have the effect of stopping the bleeding.'

'Could the man have shot himself?' said Inspector Pepper.

'No,' answered the police doctor. 'The shot must have been fired from a range of at least four yards.'

'Then we can wash out suicide,' said Pepper, and looked at Gallers. 'You were the first to discover the crime, I believe. I should like you to tell me exactly how you came to make the discovery.'

Gallers told him, and the inspector listened, interrupting every now and again with a question. 'Well, it's very peculiar, very peculiar, indeed,' he remarked, when the Scotland Yard man had finished. 'Here's a man shot, and there's nobody else in the room when the shot is fired, according to Inspector Galler's story. Where was the rest of the household?'

'Most of us were having breakfast in the dining room,' said Colonel Shand. 'All of us, in fact, except Mrs. Ramsden, Miss Weston, and Inspector Gallers.'

'So with the exception of those three,' said Inspector Pepper, frowning, 'and the servants, everybody's got an alibi.'

'That's correct,' nodded the Chief Constable.

'Well, before we go any further,' said the inspector, 'I'd just like to find out what these two ladies and the servants were doing at the time the shot was fired. You might send for them, sir, will you?'

Shand rang for the butler, and when he arrived sent for the rest of the servants. They came, a rather frightened little bunch, and Inspector Pepper began his interrogations. With the exception of the kitchen maid, who had been in the scullery, they had all heard the shot. Hollick, the butler, had been talking to the cook. Elsie, the housemaid, had just taken up Mrs. Ramsden's breakfast. Nora, the second housemaid, had been in the bathroom preparing a bath for Lucy Weston. Except for the shot none of them had seen or heard anything suspicious. Elsie had taken up Mr. Mortimer's early cup of tea at eight o'clock and he had then been up and partially dressed.

Pepper tried to shake these various statements, but without result, and finally the servants were dismissed.

Mrs. Ramsden and Lucy Weston, when they came, confirmed the statements of the two housemaids. Elsie, at the time when the shot startled her, Mrs. Ramsden affirmed, had just brought in her breakfast. Lucy Weston stated that Nora had just left the room to prepare her bath when she heard the sound of a report.

'Well, that accounts for everybody,' said Inspector Pepper, scratching his head, when they were once more standing in Mortimer's bedroom. 'And so far as I can see none of them could have committed the crime.'

He made a search of the body, but beyond the ordinary things that one would have expected to find in the pockets there was nothing of interest. A wallet containing some money and some stamps, a few visiting cards and two business letters; a gold watch and chain, eighteen shillings in silver and copper, a bunch of keys and a gold cigarette case with a lighter to match were all.

'There's no clue there,' said Pepper, shaking his head disappointedly. 'We may as well move him onto the bed now.' With the help of the constable they lifted the dead man, laid him on the bed and covered him with a sheet.

'Well,' he said, when this had been done, 'at the present moment, on the evidence that has been placed before me, there is only one person, so far as I can see, who could have committed the crime.'

'To whom are you referring?' asked Shand uneasily.

The inspector looked at him steadily.

'I'm referring to Inspector Gallers,' he said.

'Me?' cried Gallers. 'What the devil do you mean?'

'You're the only person in this house who hasn't got an alibi,' said Pepper sternly. 'On your evidence you admit that no one could have left the room between the time you heard the shot and the time you discovered the body.'

'You're talking a lot of drivel,' said the Scotland Yard man angrily. 'Why should I want to kill Mortimer — '

'I don't know that, and I'm not, of course, stating that you did,' interrupted Pepper significantly. 'But there was obviously something between you, the note he wrote proves that, and you can't get away from the fact that you were the only person who had the opportunity of committing the crime.'

'You're not serious, Pepper, surely!' exclaimed Colonel Shand. 'Inspector Gallers is a well-known official at Scotland Yard.'

'If he was the Home Secretary, sir,' said the inspector, with dignity, 'it would be my duty to investigate his connection with the dead man. Of course, if you officially instruct me not to, that's a different matter.'

The Chief Constable bit his lip. Inspector Pepper was perfectly right and he knew it. Gallers' position certainly did not seem very clear. Shand's duty as Chief Constable of the county, came before his duty as a host.

'I'm sorry,' he said, turning to the Scotland Yard man, 'but I'm afraid I can't interfere. As you yourself must realize, Inspector Pepper is merely carrying out his duty.'

Gallers nodded.

'You're quite right, Colonel,' he said. 'It's all nonsense, of course, but if I were in the inspector's place I should do the same.'

Two seconds later he was officially warned that as a material witness he would be required throughout the rest of the investigation, and would be detained under police supervision. Before he left, with the triumphant Pepper, for certain formalities at the station, Mr. Whipple managed to get a word with him alone.

'This is — this is really very dreadful,' he said. 'I don't know how to express my — my — my sorrow that this should have happened. Perhaps I — I may be able to do something.' He was a little incoherent, but Gallers realized what he meant.

'Thank you, Mr. Whipple,' he said. 'But I'm afraid you'll find it will be a difficult job.'

The little man nodded miserably. Not even he realized how difficult it was going to be.

5

INTERLUDE

Luncheon that day was not a very cheerful meal. The two vacant places previously occupied by Mortimer and Gallers were grim reminders of the tragedy that had cast its shadow over the whole house. Even the jovial Ramsden was gloomy and depressed and for the most part ate in silence, without raising his eyes from his plate.

By tacit consent the subject of the crime was not mentioned. What small amount of conversation there was, was religiously kept to trivial topics, and since nobody present was the least bit interested in anything but the murder which had been committed in their midst, this was patchy and disjointed, and eventually drifted to almost complete silence.

When, to everybody's relief, the meal was over, Mr. Whipple took Shand aside.

'I'd — I'd like to have a — a word or two with you in private,' he said diffidently.

The worried Chief Constable nodded.

'Come into the library,' he answered. 'We shan't be disturbed there.'

When they were seated in the comfortable book-lined room and the door had been shut, Mr. Whipple polished his glasses and perched himself on the edge of an armchair.

'This is a very unfortunate business,' he began. 'There's no doubt that — er — that things do look very black indeed against Gallers. If I didn't know him as well as I do I think I should be — er — rather of the same opinion as Inspector Pepper. But since I'm convinced that Gallers is as innocent as you or I, I think I should like to try and find out the truth.'

'How do you propose to start?' enquired Shand doubtfully. This insignificant little man before him had, on one occasion, succeeded in solving a murder mystery, but the Chief Constable had always been under the impression that luck, more than anything else, had been the reason for that success.

'By trying to discover a motive for the murder,' replied Mr. Whipple. 'I am sure you will agree with me that at the moment that is the weakest part of the evidence against Inspector Gallers.' He moistened his lips. 'In this, I am hoping, you may be able to help me. How long have you known Mortimer?'

Shand considered.

'Roughly about three years,' he answered. 'I met him first at the golf club and we became friendly. He only lives about fifteen miles away, at Long Hatton.'

'Did you — did you know anything about him?' continued Mr. Whipple

'Very little,' admitted the Chief Constable. 'He was rather a reserved man and never spoke about himself. I gathered though, in one way and another, that he had retired from business and was fairly well-off.'

'What *was* his business?' enquired Mr. Whipple with interest.

Shand shook his head.

'I don't know,' he answered. 'I've often wondered myself.'

'Was he married?' asked the little man.

'No, a bachelor,' replied the Colonel. 'I don't think he had any relations at all. If he had he never mentioned them.'

'It appears,' said Mr. Whipple, wrinkling his forehead, 'that he was a little — er — mysterious.'

'In a way he was,' agreed Shand. 'I know quite a lot of people who didn't like him, but that was his manner, he was always rather brusque and offhand. He gave me the impression that he'd had a lot of trouble.' Mr. Whipple looked at him quickly.

'What sort of trouble?' he asked.

'I don't know.' The Chief Constable stroked his grey moustache. 'But I think he must have led rather a hard life in his youth. He never actually said so, but I gathered it from one or two remarks he let drop.'

There was a pause, during which Mr. Whipple gently rubbed the bridge of his nose.

'Is that — is that all you can tell me about him?' he said at last, and Shand smiled a little wryly.

'I'm afraid it is,' he confessed.

'You can think of — er — nothing,' persisted the little man, 'that would be likely to suggest a reason for his being killed?'

'Nothing,' declared the Colonel emphatically. 'So far as his private life was concerned I knew absolutely nothing!'

Not very illuminating, thought Mr. Whipple dejectedly. Perhaps there would be a lawyer or someone who might be able to supply further information regarding the dead man. He made a mental note to try and discover this at the first available opportunity.

Coming out of the library he ran into Jackson. The ex-inspector was looking serious and depressed, but he forced a smile as he caught sight of Mr. Whipple.

'Hello!' he greeted. 'I hear that you're going to try and clear up this dreadful business.'

'Really — er — I — I'm going to do what I can,' said Mr. Whipple; acutely embarrassed. 'I must admit I haven't got very far at the moment.'

'It's pretty awful for poor Gallers,' said

Jackson, shaking his head. 'Of course he hadn't anything to do with the murder, the local man's a fool!'

'I can't say that I like Inspector Pepper,' said Mr. Whipple, 'but I don't think he's a fool, by any means.'

'I suppose you're right,' admitted the ex-inspector, 'and anyway, Gallers is only detained on suspicion. You haven't any ideas — formed any theories — ' He left the sentence unfinished and looked at the other questioningly.

Mr. Whipple shook his head.

'None at the moment, I'm afraid,' he answered, despondently.

'Well, if you want any help,' said Jackson, 'you'll call on me, won't you? I'd like to do anything I can to help old Gallers.'

Mr. Whipple promised, and leaving the ex-inspector went up the stairs to his room. Lighting the gas fire he pulled an armchair in front of it and sat down to think the whole thing out.

Taking it for granted that Gallers was innocent, who could have fired the shot that killed Mortimer? And having fired it how, in the short time between the report and Gallers finding of the body could they have got away? Escape by the door was impossible, for Gallers was in sight of that when the shot had been fired. The window was equally as impossible. Nobody could have left that way without disturbing the snow on the sill. Therefore, on the face of it, the whole thing was impossible, and yet somebody had fired that shot and the question was — how?

With knitted brows the little draper tried to arrive at some satisfactory solution, or even hit on the basis of a theory upon which he could build. At the end of a quarter of an hour he was still as barren of ideas as he had been when he sat down. Apart from the utter impossibility of there having been anybody in the room when the shot had killed Mortimer, there was nobody in the house, with the exception of Gallers, who could have been there, even providing the difficulty of how they got away could have been overcome. Everyone else had an alibi. Mr. Whipple ran over them to check them up.

Egerton, Shand, Ramsden, Dick and

Jackson had been in the dining room. There was no argument about that, he had seen them there himself. Mrs. Ramsden had been in her bedroom; the housemaid, Elsie, had been with her so they each supplied the other's alibi. Lucy Weston had been alone but Nora, the other housemaid had only just left her to prepare her bath. That left Claire Weston. Now, where was Claire Weston? Oh yes, Mr. Whipple remembered, she had been in the dining room, too. The rest of the servants had been in the kitchen. So, ruling out Gallers, nobody in the house *could* have shot Mortimer.

Now was it possible for anybody *outside* the house to have done it? But for the fact that the shot had definitely been fired from inside the room it would have been quite possible for somebody to have killed Mortimer as he stood at the open window. And yet, would it? Unconsciously, Mr. Whipple shook his head. No definitely, it would not. In the first place, the bullet would have been found in the room, and there had been no sign of it; and in the second place, unless the murderer had been up in a balloon, the angle was all wrong. The bullet had struck Mortimer between the eyes, passed through the head and come out at the base of the skull. No, the outside idea could be discarded; and anyway, there was the sound of the shot and the smell of the cordite, which definitely discounted any such suggestion.

Mr. Whipple rubbed his forehead despondently. This was really a very tough problem — there were such a lot of impossibilities to be got over. Searching for a new line of attack, he remembered the piece of coal in Mortimer's hand. Was there anything significant in that? Why had it been in the dead man's hand, and how had it come into his possession? There was no coal in his room, and yet he had died with that lump clasped firmly in his fingers.

He puzzled over this for some time, and eventually gave it up with a sigh. He could think of no practical suggestion that would account for its presence. What else was there that might provide him with a clue? The snow! The snow, which had been white and turned red!

That was a peculiar phenomenon that had yet to be explained. There was no doubt that the redness was blood, and still less that the blood had come from the wound in Mortimer's head. But why had the snow been white when he had first looked out of that window, and red when he and Gallers had later gone down to look for any traces? The wound had not bled in the meanwhile, that was certain, and yet the snow had turned from white to red!

Mr. Whipple thought until his head ached. There was a simple explanation, of course, but what was it? And then quite suddenly he sat up with an exclamation, his eyes gleaming. Was the idea that had suddenly come to him, absurd? That simple idea, which explained the unexplainable. Or was it the solution of the whole mystery?

6

A LUMP OF COAL

It was at half-past two when that startling idea which was eventually to lead Mr. Whipple to the amazing truth occurred to him, and he set to work immediately to test his theory. It all rested on one small item of information. If this was what he expected it to be — what his imagination told him it must be — then the whole viewpoint of the crime was changed.

Making his way downstairs he went in search of Hollick and found the butler in his pantry, reading the morning paper.

'I'm extremely sorry to disturb you, Hollick,' said Mr. Whipple nervously, 'but I would like a word with you, if you don't mind.'

The butler laid aside his paper, removed his glasses, and rose to his feet.

'Yes, sir?' he said, expectantly.

'I'm going to ask you a question,' said

Mr. Whipple, 'and I want you to think very carefully, Hollick, before you answer it. A — a great deal may depend on what you say.'

The butler's scanty eyebrows went up slightly.

'Yes, sir?' he said again, and waited.

Mr. Whipple put his question, and rather to his surprise, the butler answered promptly.

'Just before nine-thirty, sir,' he said. 'To be exact — nine-twenty-eight.'

'You are — er — certain of that?' queried Mr. Whipple, suppressing his excitement.

Hollick inclined his head.

'Absolutely, sir,' he declared emphatically. 'I particularly noticed it because at the time I was looking for the butcher's boy, who was late.'

'Dear me, how very interesting,' murmured Mr. Whipple. 'And would you be prepared to swear to the time, Hollick? It's very important.'

'I should be prepared to swear to it, sir,' answered the butler gravely. 'I had just looked at my watch.'

'Thank you, thank you very much, Hollick,' said Mr. Whipple gratefully. 'What you have told me is going to be a great help. Now I should like — er — I should like you to keep this conversation to yourself, if you wouldn't mind.'

'Certainly, sir,' replied Hollick, with dignity. 'I seldom indulge in gossip.'

Mr. Whipple left him with a feeling of exhilaration. He had got the information he wanted and with less trouble than he had expected. He blessed the lateness of the butcher's boy, but there was still a lot to be done. What Hollick had been able to tell him had only proved that his theory was materially possible. He had still to turn that possibility into certainty.

Hurrying up the stairs again, he walked along the corridor to the room in which Mortimer had met his death. It was only when he reached the door and his hand was on the handle that he remembered that Inspector Pepper had locked it and taken the key away with him.

He frowned and rubbed his chin. It was essential that he should have another look inside that room. The key could be sent for, of course. On the Chief Constable's authority the inspector would deliver it up, but that would mean delay and a certain amount of publicity and just then he did not want either.

It occurred to him that it was more than possible that one of the other keys would fit the lock. He tried the key from the room next door, and to his delight it turned easily. Slipping into the room he closed the door behind him and locked it.

The apartment was exactly as it had been in the morning. The sheeted figure of the dead man still lay on the bed, silent and motionless. It was icy cold up here, for the window had been left open. For a few moments Mr. Whipple stood just inside the entrance and allowed his eyes to wander slowly around the apartment. Where would be the most likely place to find the thing he was looking for? He decided that it might be anywhere, but that it was in the room somewhere he was sure. The murderer could have had neither the time nor the opportunity to remove it.

He began a close and thorough

examination, crawling under the bed and looking in drawers and cupboards and even under the seats of the chairs, but he failed to find what he was searching for, and yet reason told him that it must be here somewhere. Taken in conjunction with the butler's statement it was the only reasonable explanation of the mystery. He tried the walls, tapping them, on the chance that there might be some secret compartment or cupboard. The house was an old one, and at the time it had been built such things were fairly common, but he could find nothing of the sort.

His heart sank a little as he paused in his labours and looked about him, pulling at his lower lip with finger and thumb. Unless he could find some trace of this thing he was looking for his whole theory fell to the ground.

His eyes, roving about, suddenly came to rest on the fireplace. That was the only portion of the room that was left, but it hardly looked likely to yield any results. The chimney and grate had been fastened up when the gas-fire had been installed and the hearth was clean and spotless. There might, however, be something in the narrow space beneath the stove itself; and going over Mr. Whipple knelt down and raked with his hand beneath it. He brought out a considerable amount of dust and dirt but nothing else, and he was just on the point of rising to his feet again when a tiny, white object amongst the litter caught his eye, and he picked it up.

As he looked at it he felt his pulse beating faster. It was the thing he had been searching for.

Carrying it over to the window, he examined it more closely. Yes, there could be no doubt. This was how the trick had been done. So far, his startling theory was being borne out. It was clever — fiendishly clever — and but for one thing over which the murderer had had no control it would, in all probability, have been undiscovered.

He put the little object carefully away in his pocket and stood thoughtfully by the open window. If he could account for the piece of coal he had found in Mortimer's hand, he had got the 'how' of the crime cut and dried. The coal, however, was one of the pieces of the puzzle that wouldn't fit. Of what use had it been in the scheme of murder?

With knitted brows he stared out at the expanse of snow-covered ground. Having got so far, he ought to be able to account for that annoying piece of coal, but, rack his brains as he might, he couldn't. Presently he leaned out of the window and looked down the side of the house at the ground below. The patch of blood was still clearly visible, but by now the air had affected it and it was not so red as it had been. He gazed at it for some time and then withdrew his head. In doing so his shoulder caught one side of the latticed window and swung it shut. He put out his hand to push it open again and as he did so he caught sight of something that caused him to catch his breath sharply. Holding the window shut, he leaned out of the other half and peered at the leaded panes. The mark he had seen through the glass was now more plainly visible. He touched it gently with his finger and, looking at the tip, he saw that it was blackened.

Had someone thrown that lump of coal at Mortimer's window, and was the mark on the glass where it had struck? In that event, how had the lump come into Mortimer's hand? In the natural course of events, after striking the pane, it would have rebounded and fallen to the ground below, for the sill was not broad enough to catch it. But it hadn't done that. It had, in some extraordinary manner, found its way into Mortimer's hand.

Mr. Whipple sighed. It was really very difficult. He felt that the explanation was within his grasp but just eluded him. The piece of coal had, without much doubt, been thrown at the window with the object, apparently, of attracting Mortimer's attention, but what had been behind that object? The man had definitely not been shot from outside.

Mr. Whipple left the window, crossed the room, and opening the door passed out into the corridor. Re-locking the door behind him, he returned the key to the next door lock, went downstairs and out of the house. A minute or two later he was standing under the window of the room he had just left. A thaw had set in, and the snow, no longer crisp, was wet and mushy. He examined the bloodstains. Mortimer must have lost a great deal of blood; and looking up, Mr. Whipple visualized the dead man as he and Gallers had found him.

With his mind's eye he could see Mortimer's head and shoulders protruding from the window and suddenly, like the switching on of a light in a dark room, he understood the whole thing; understood why that piece of coal had been in the dead man's hand and just *how* he had met his death!

For the next ten minutes he was very busy indeed, and when at last he re-entered the house there was a little smile on his lips. He knew just *how* that impossible crime had been committed, all that remained now was *why*, and by *whom*!

7

THE SNIPER

When he entered the drawing room he found part of the house party sitting round the fire. John Ramsden was leaning back in a big armchair and from the rhythmic sounds that were proceeding from his open mouth, he was obviously asleep. His wife, sitting near him, was talking in low tones to Lucy Weston; and Dick, by the window, was showing Claire a portfolio of etchings. Ex-Detective Inspector Jackson was sucking on the point of a pencil and frowning over a folded newspaper on his knee, evidently in the midst of trying to solve a crossword puzzle. He looked up as Mr. Whipple came in.

'Hello!' he said. 'Where have you been?'

'I — er — well, I've been rather busy,' answered the little man.

Mrs. Ramsden smiled.

'Sure you haven't been doing the same as John?' she said, nodding towards the sleeping novelist. 'He'll say that when he wakes up. He never sleeps — it's always thinking with him.'

'No, really, I have been busy,' protested Mr. Whipple. 'Have — er — have any of you seen our host?'

'He's in the library, I think,' said Dick.

Jackson put down his paper and crossed over to Mr. Whipple's side.

'Have you discovered anything?' he asked, in a low voice.

'I'm — er — I'm afraid not,' said Mr. Whipple untruthfully. 'That is to say I haven't — er — proved anything yet. You say Colonel Shand is in the library?'

'That's where father said he was going,' called Dick, from the window.

'Thank you, thank you very much,' said the little man hastily. 'I'll go and hunt him out.'

He left the drawing room with a sigh of relief and crossed the hall to the library. A murmur of voices came from the partly open door and when he looked in he found Egerton and Shand holding a heated argument concerning the government of the country. The two men looked round as they heard the door open, and Shand broke off in the middle of his argument.

'Do you want me, Whipple?' he asked.

'Well — er — really — er — I'm sorry to intrude, but if you can spare a minute,' said Mr. Whipple.

With a word of apology to Egerton, the Chief Constable came over to his side.

'What is it?' he asked eagerly. 'You've found something?'

'I really don't know,' said Mr. Whipple. 'I think possibly I may have — Which is the quickest way to Mortimer's house?'

'Mortimer's house?' repeated Shand, raising his eyebrows. 'You go straight through the village and turn to the left till you come to the main road, and then you take the second on your right. It's rather difficult to explain. Are you thinking of going?'

'I *am* going,' corrected Mr. Whipple. 'What I wanted was to know if you'd be so very kind as to give me a note to

Inspector Pepper authorizing him to — er — to let me look over the house.'

'I'll do better than that,' said the Colonel quickly, 'I'll come with you. When do you want to go?'

'I should like to go now,' said Mr. Whipple apologetically.

'Right you are,' said the Chief Constable. 'I'll go and tell Dick I'm going out. Put on a coat and I'll be ready.'

'This is most kind of you,' said Mr. Whipple, and he moved towards the drawing room door.

The Colonel was following him when he remembered his guest.

'By jove!' he muttered. 'I suppose I'd better tell Egerton I'm not coming back. Can't leave him there like that.'

He went back and re-entered the library, and Mr. Whipple waited for him, thoughtfully biting the end of his thumb.

The greyness of the December evening was beginning to fall when Shand brought his car to a halt at the front entrance of James Mortimer's square, ugly house. A police constable opened the door in answer to his ring, and recognizing Shand saluted.

'You want to see Inspector Pepper, sir?' said the man. 'He's upstairs now.'

'Who's that, Barlow?' enquired Pepper's voice from somewhere above.

'Colonel Shand, sir,' said the constable.

There was the sound of quick footsteps on the stair and Inspector Pepper came hurrying down.

'Good evening, sir,' he said. 'The sergeant and I have just come over to make a search of the place to see if we can find anything that will supply us with a motive for the crime.' He rather rudely ignored Mr. Whipple entirely.

'You've been rather a long time about it, haven't you?' said the Chief Constable.

The inspector's thin face flushed.

'The dead man had sent his servants away over the weekend, sir,' he replied, 'and we had to find his housekeeper before we could get the keys.'

'I see,' Shand nodded thoughtfully. 'Well, Mr. Whipple would like to be present while you conduct the search.'

The inspector let his eyes rest for a

moment on the insignificant figure of the little draper before he replied.

'That is as you wish, sir,' he said. 'We are beginning with the study. Perhaps you will come up.'

He led the way up the stairs to a broad landing and opened a door on the right, ushering them into a large room, which was comfortably furnished as a study. Mortimer had evidently been a man with an eye for comfort. The carpet was of thick pile and fitted closely to the skirting board. One side of the room was completely covered with bookshelves, crammed with odd volumes. By the window was a large roll-top desk, and drawn up by the fireplace were two big, brown leather chairs. The desk was open, and seated at it was a thick-set man, whom Pepper introduced as Sergeant Scales.

'How far have you got with the search?' asked Shand.

'Only just started,' grunted the inspector.

'I see you've brought the dead man's keys with you,' ventured Mr. Whipple, pointing to the bunch that still dangled in the keyhole of the desk. 'How was it — er — since you were in possession of the keys that you — er — had to find the housekeeper before you could gain admission?'

'There was no key to the house on the bunch,' answered Pepper shortly.

Mr. Whipple raised his eyebrows.

'Dear me, no key?' he said softly. 'Really, don't you think that's extremely peculiar, Inspector?'

The inspector shot him a quick glance.

'I don't know,' he answered ungraciously. 'Perhaps he never carried one, lots of gentlemen don't.'

'Did you — er — ask the housekeeper?' said Mr. Whipple.

'No I didn't,' growled Pepper. 'I didn't think it was necessary.'

'I — er — I should very much like to know whether he was in the habit of carrying a key,' murmured the little man, frowning.

'Why?' enquired Shand. 'D'you think it's important?'

'Dear me, no, it's not important,'

answered Mr. Whipple, 'but — er — I should just like to know, because if he left the house *with* a front door key on that ring it would be — er — it would be interesting to discover what happened to it.'

'The housekeeper's downstairs,' said the inspector. 'I'll get Barlow to ask her.' He called to the constable. 'Barlow,' he said, 'go and ask Mrs. Kelp if Mr. Mortimer was in the habit of carrying a latch-key.'

'Right, sir,' answered the faint voice of the constable from below.

The inspector came back again into the room.

'Now then, Scales,' he said, 'we'll get on with this search.' The tone of his voice implied that he had had enough interruptions.

While he and the sergeant were going through the papers on the desk, Mr. Whipple stood and watched them, peering short-sightedly through his spectacles. James Mortimer had, apparently, been a methodical man; everything had been done up neatly in bundles, docketed and stowed away in its appropriate pigeonhole. They found a number of receipted bills, mostly concerning household expenses, a few that hadn't been paid and a number of documents relating to various industrial concerns. There were several prospectuses of new companies. In one of the pigeonholes was a long list of securities, which had been neatly typewritten; and against them, in the margin, there were a few pencilled notes. In one of the drawers of the desk they found a file containing a number of business letters, mostly from a firm of brokers, concerning the buying and selling of shares. Mortimer had evidently kept a keen eye on the market, but had not indulged in any wild speculations. The firm of brokers he had dealt with was an old-established one, and his dealings had been of the soundest. There were no private letters of any kind. Either he hadn't received any or they had been destroyed as soon as he had read them. There was a cashbook in which the dead man had kept an account of his income and expenditure, and this was the only thing that was at all illuminating.

Up to three years ago the expenditure had been very modest, and then suddenly there appeared large monthly sums, which had been paid out to some unknown person represented by 'X'.

It started with 'X, £200'. This went on for a year, and then the sum changed to £400, and after a month or two to £1,000, and recently to £2,000.

'Here's the motive,' said Inspector Pepper, with satisfaction. 'Blackmail! Someone must have been squeezing Mortimer because he knew something against him.'

'And so — er — he shoots the goose that lays the golden eggs,' remarked Mr. Whipple, and shook his head. 'That doesn't appear to be a very good motive to me, Inspector. If it was the other way round it would, of course, be different. It's understandable if Mortimer — er — shot the person who was putting the — er — the screw on him, but not the other way.'

'Well, there you are, it happened,'

grunted Pepper. 'Probably Mortimer got fed up and threatened go to the police. That would provide us with sufficient motive for his being killed.'

Mr. Whipple uttered an exclamation and a little gleam came into his eye.

'Really, you know, I believe you've hit it,' he said. 'Yes, yes, undoubtedly that is why he sent that note to Gallers.'

'You mean he didn't know who'd been putting the 'black' on him?' said Pepper, 'and sent the note to the very man he was going to give away?'

'Dear me, no. I mean nothing of the sort,' said Mr. Whipple. 'Inspector Gallers did not shoot Mr. Mortimer, I'm certain of that.'

'Are you,' said Pepper. 'Well, I think you'll have difficulty in proving it.'

Before Mr. Whipple could reply, there came a tap at the door and the constable entered.

'The housekeeper, sir,' he said, 'says that Mr. Mortimer always carried a latchkey on the bunch in his pocket.'

'All right, Barlow,' said Pepper, and the man withdrew.

The Chief Constable glanced at Mr. Whipple.

'What do you make of that?' he asked.

The little man shrugged his shoulders.

'It would seem the murderer must have taken it off the bunch after he had — er — killed Mortimer,' he replied, and then rather abruptly changing the subject: 'Is there — er — is there anything else in that desk?'

There was nothing else in the desk beyond a quantity of envelopes and writing paper.

'Nothing more here,' growled Pepper, 'and there's no other place in the room where he's likely to keep papers. We'd best try the bedroom.'

Sergeant Scales rose and followed him to the door. The inspector turned on the threshold and looked back. He had expected Mr. Whipple to accompany them, but that gentleman was standing by the side of the open desk gently pulling his nose, and apparently completely lost in thought. Pepper looked at him for a moment, and then shrugging his shoulders resignedly went out, followed by the sergeant.

'Aren't you going with them?' asked Shand.

Mr. Whipple shook his head.

'No — er — really, thanks,' he answered. 'I'm still interested in this desk. It's the same make as my own, and — er — there should be an alleged secret drawer behind the two shallow drawers under the pigeonholes.'

He pulled the right one out as he spoke and felt about in the place where it had been with his fingers. There was a gentle click and a part of the back of the desk sprang forward an inch. He grasped it and lifted it completely away.

'I thought so,' he murmured with satisfaction.

Behind where the false back had been was a long, narrow drawer, and as he opened it the Chief Constable bent eagerly forward. It contained a mass of newspaper cuttings: there were some two dozen of them in all, and the yellowness of the paper proclaimed their age.

Mr. Whipple peered at the glaring headlines and the photograph on the top one and his lips opened in an 'O' of astonishment.

'So that was James Mortimer's secret,' he said.

The photograph was a photograph of James Mortimer — a much younger edition, it was true, but still undeniably James Mortimer — but the name under it was 'James Flagg'.

'By jove!' breathed Shand. 'I remember the Flagg case.'

'I am familiar with it, too,' said Mr. Whipple. 'I have a full account of it amongst my collection of famous trials.'

He knew now why his first meeting with James Mortimer had stirred a responsive chord in his memory, why the man's face had seemed vaguely familiar. There, in those glaring black headlines, lay the answer.

James Flagg had been the Managing Director of the Atlas Textile Corporation, Limited, and after a long trial had been found guilty of embezzling the company's funds to the extent of nearly seventy-five thousand pounds. He had been sentenced to a term of five years' penal servitude and, but for a particularly clever counsel, his sentence would have been far heavier. This had occurred fifteen years previously.

'So that's why he was being blackmailed,' said Shand. 'That's the story He served his sentence, came out and started in business under another name. Made money and settled down here as James Mortimer. Somebody either knew or found out that he was Flagg and threatened to make the matter public unless he paid up. He'd established a decent reputation in the neighbourhood and probably was sensitive at the idea of being exposed, and paid sooner than lose his respectability.'

'The — er — the majority of people would do the same under the same circumstances,' said Mr. Whipple. 'It's an extraordinary thing, Colonel Shand, the number of people who have committed crimes in order to be thought respectable.'

'And this wasn't a question of crime, it was a question of money,' said the Colonel. 'I suppose he got fed up with paying out towards the end and threatened his persecutor with the law. We know he contemplated doing so, that partly finished letter which he started and then discarded proves that. He was probably in the act of writing it when he remembered that Gallers represented the law and sent the note to him with the intention of telling him the whole story.'

'And he was killed to prevent that,' murmured Mr. Whipple.

'Exactly!' agreed Shand. 'But who could have killed him and how?'

'I think,' the little man took off his glasses and polished them nervously. 'I think I — I may shortly be in a position to tell you that,' he said.

'You know — ' began Shand.

'Nearly everything,' interrupted Mr. Whipple gently, and at that moment the inspector and Sergeant Scales came back.

'There's nothing in the bedroom,' said the inspector. 'We're going to have a look over the rest of the house now.'

'Before you do that, Inspector,' said Shand, picking up the sheaf of newspaper cuttings and holding them out, 'you'd better have a look at these, they'll probably interest you.'

Pepper took them, glanced at the headlines and the photograph, and his small eyes opened wide.

'What's this, what's this?' he muttered. 'Where did you find these?'

'Mr. Whipple found them in the desk,' answered the Chief Constable. 'There was a secret drawer at the back which you overlooked.'

'Well, this shows why he was being blackmailed,' said Pepper. 'The case is almost complete now.'

'I think it is,' murmured Mr. Whipple complacently.

'Oh, so you're beginning to come round to my way of thinking, are you?' said the inspector. 'I'm glad to hear that.'

'I wasn't,' said Mr. Whipple, 'referring to — er — *your* case. I was referring to — er — *mine*.'

'Yours?' Pepper stared at him.

'Mine!' repeated Mr. Whipple grimly. 'I only require one more piece of information and it is complete.'

'I don't understand you,' muttered Pepper.

'You will,' said Mr. Whipple, and with great deliberation pulled out his watch. 'If you — er — could make it convenient to come to Longford Chase at nine o'clock tonight and bring Detective Inspector Gallers with you I will — er — introduce to you the — er — murderer.'

'You'll what?' cried Pepper, and laughed.

'I think you'd better come, Pepper,' said the Chief Constable.

The inspector shrugged his shoulders,

'If you order me to, sir,' he said, 'that's a different matter.' He looked at Mr. Whipple disparagingly. 'Nine o'clock, you said?'

'Nine o'clock precisely!' said Mr. Whipple. 'And would you mind telling me, is there a telephone in this house?'

'Yes, sir,' answered Sergeant Scales. 'In a little lobby off the hall.'

'Then — er — if you will excuse me,' said Mr. Whipple apologetically, 'I'll — er — just go and use it I want to — er — put a call through.'

He left them, and hurrying downstairs

discovered the lobby to the right of the front door, and when he returned and joined Shand there was an expression of satisfaction on his face.

They took their leave of Inspector Pepper and went back to the waiting car.

'Did you mean what you said just now?' asked Shand, as they drove back.

'Dear me, yes, of course,' replied Mr. Whipple. 'There were, you see, three questions to answer: how, why and who. I found the answer to the first this afternoon, and I've — er — just discovered the answer to the other two.'

Before the Chief Constable could put the question which was hovering on his lips, Mr. Whipple went on:

'There is one favour I wish you would grant me. Could you let me have a list of the bedrooms and who occupies them?'

'I don't quite understand you,' said the Chief Constable.

'Really — er — I'm afraid I'm not very good at making my meaning clear,' said Mr. Whipple. 'What I want to know is, where everyone was sleeping last night.'

He relapsed into silence, and did not

speak again until they were on the point of turning into the drive at Longford Chase, and then he said:

'I feel that it would be — er — better — er — if we didn't let anybody in the house know what we found this afternoon.'

'I shan't say anything,' said Shand, 'but I must say you're deuced mysterious, Whipple — '

His words were drowned in a sharp report and a crash of breaking glass. The windscreen shivered to fragments and something thudded into the frame of the window behind Mr. Whipple's head. The Chief Constable brought the car to a jarring halt.

'What the devil was that?' he gasped.

'I think it was a bullet,' murmured Mr. Whipple gently, and even as the words left his lips the second shot smashed the left side window.

This time they saw the flash. It came from a clump of bushes at the side of the drive. Shand wrenched open the door and sprang out. As he did so a third bullet whistled past his head. He raced in the direction from which the shot had come, but when he reached the clump of bushes there was nobody there. He heard the sound of retreating footsteps, and the snapping of branches as the sniper forced his way through the shrubbery, and he went in pursuit. But it was dark, and presently he realized that the other must have eluded him, for now he could hear nothing. He paused and listened intently, but there was no sound; and realizing that it was useless to attempt to follow the man further, he made his way back to the car.

Mr. Whipple had alighted and was peering anxiously towards him.

'Did you lose him?' he asked.

Shand nodded.

'Yes, he slipped me in the darkness of the shrubbery,' he answered. 'I wonder who it was?'

'I don't wonder,' said Mr. Whipple softly. 'I know!'

8

SUSPENSE

Leaving the car to be taken round to the garage, they walked up the remainder of the drive to the house. The sound of the shots had evidently been heard and caused some alarm, for the front door was open and Hollick was standing at the top of the steps, staring into the darkness. Behind him, in the lighted hall, they caught a glimpse of Dick, John Ramsden and the three women, looking anxiously towards the door.

'What were those shots, Father?' asked Dick, as Shand and Mr. Whipple came up the steps.

'Somebody — er — mistook us for rabbits,' replied the little man, before the Colonel could speak. 'There's no damage done, luckily, except, I'm afraid, to your car.'

'Who was it?' asked John Ramsden.

'We didn't see the shooter,' answered the Chief Constable. 'He was hiding in the bushes at the side of the drive.'

As they crossed the hall, Jackson appeared in the door of the library, pencil and paper in his hand.

'What happened?' he enquired, catching Mr. Whipple by the arm.

In a low voice that was inaudible to the others, he explained.

'Good God!' The ex-inspector's face was grave. 'What was the idea?'

'I think,' said Mr. Whipple, 'the idea was to shoot *me*. Er — Inspector Jackson, this afternoon you offered very kindly to help. Is that offer still open?'

'Of course!' said Jackson, eagerly. 'What can I do?'

'If you wouldn't mind coming up to my room just before dinner,' murmured Mr. Whipple.

Jackson nodded, and the little man went on up the stairs. Reaching his room, he rang the bell. Elsie answered the summons and he asked her to bring him some tea. After he had sipped it gratefully, he began to dress leisurely for dinner. He was fumbling uncertainly with his tie when there came a tap at the door, and in answer to his invitation Jackson entered.

'What have you to tell me, Mr. Whipple?' he asked.

Mr. Whipple carefully patted the ends of his tie neatly into position and adjusted his dinner jacket before he answered.

'I think,' he said, 'there may be some kind of — er — of — er — trouble here tonight. I want you to keep — er — an eye on Mr. Egerton.'

The ex-inspector's face was the picture of amazement.

'Egerton?' he repeated blankly. 'You surely don't suspect — '

'Dear me, no,' broke in Mr. Whipple. 'I don't suspect anything — I know.'

'But how did he do it?' said Jackson.

'That I'll tell you later,' answered Mr. Whipple. 'That's why I want you to help me. After dinner I — er — I propose to explain just how this crime was committed, and I want you to keep close to Egerton while I'm doing it.'

'Do you think he'll turn nasty?' said Jackson.

'I — I think it's highly probable,' answered the other. 'By — by the way, are you armed?'

The ex-inspector shook his head.

'Then you'd better take this,' said Mr. Whipple. He picked up an automatic pistol gingerly and held it out. 'I took it from the gun-room,' he said. 'Be careful, it's loaded.'

Jackson took it and dropped it into his pocket, and at that moment the dinner gong boomed.

'Dear me,' said Mr. Whipple, 'that sounds very welcome. We'll go down.'

The meal started almost as gloomily as had lunch, but by the end of the second course things had brightened up considerably. This was due mostly to the efforts of Colonel Shand, who kept up a running fire of conversation. Stories and anecdotes fell from his lips in a constant stream, and as the meal proceeded a shadow seemed to lift from the faces of the people sitting round the table.

'By the way,' said Dick suddenly, during a momentary pause, 'how do you get your plots, Ramsden?'

The novelist made a grimace.

'Sometimes I don't,' he answered.

'But when you do?' persisted Dick.

'Well,' said Ramsden thoughtfully. 'I try to get hold of a good central situation and build round it. Sometimes I start with a title, which gives me the idea for the theme of a story.'

'Dear me, that's very interesting,' said Mr. Whipple. 'I am, as you know, a great reader of detective fiction. Would you — would you mind telling us what the plot was you had — er — concocted for Inspector Gallers and myself to exercise our wits on?'

Ramsden shifted a little uneasily in his chair.

'Well I don't know why I shouldn't tell you,' he said at last. 'It was this: I made Mortimer a society blackmailer. He was blackmailing all of us, particularly Mildred.' He looked across at his wife. 'She had been married before and thought, when she married me, that her husband was dead. Mortimer, however, had discovered that he was still alive and was threatening to expose her for having committed bigamy.

In my story she was supposed to have had an interview with him during the night at which she killed him — she stabbed him, as a matter of fact, with a hatpin. I had arranged that certain clues should be left, such as a slight smear of lipstick on the body, which had got there during the struggle, for you and Gallers to follow up. But I had also provided her with an alibi because — again in my story — after killing Mortimer she had come and confessed everything to me. Of course, I provided her with an alibi and she provided me with one. There were a lot more details, but that, roughly, was the idea.'

'That's very interesting,' remarked Mr. Whipple thoughtfully. 'It's extraordinary, when you come to think of it, how different the actual occurrence was to the faked crime you planned.'

'Yes,' said John Ramsden slowly. 'I suppose it is.'

'In actual fact,' the little man went on, his eyes on his plate and crumbling his bread, 'instead of being stabbed Mortimer was shot. Instead of being a blackmailer he was, if I may coin a word, the blackmailee. Also, the person who killed him was a man and not a woman. In fact the real circumstances were almost directly opposite to your imaginative ones.'

There was silence at the table. A peculiar atmosphere had drifted into the room and everyone was feeling its effects. It was like the sudden hush before the lightning flash that heralds the approaching storm. Subconsciously they all felt that a crisis was at hand. With grave faces they stared at Mr. Whipple, causing that gentleman great uneasiness, waiting, almost breathlessly, for his next words. When they came they were in the nature of an anti-climax.

'This is — er — very excellent chicken, Colonel Shand,' he said.

A sigh ran round the table, a sigh caused by the release of pent-up breath. The tension of the atmosphere relaxed. John Ramsden rather obviously turned the conversation into a fresh channel and once again it became general, although there was at least one person present in whose heart fear was still active.

The meal came to an end at last, and just before Hollick served the coffee Mr. Whipple took his watch from his pocket and after a glance at it turned towards Shand.

'I should like, with your permission, Colonel Shand,' he said nervously, 'to suggest that we all take our coffee in the drawing room. I have — er — something to tell you. Mr. Ramsden here has just very kindly outlined his idea for the fake murder. At nine o'clock — that is in precisely three minutes' time — I propose to tell you the story of the real murder. My — er — story is not imaginative, it is fact, and when I have finished it you will know exactly how James Mortimer met his death, why he died, and the name of the person who killed him!'

9

MR. WHIPPLE TELLS HIS STORY

Rather ill at ease, Mr. Whipple took up his position by the drawing room mantelpiece and blinked nervously at the semi-circle of people grouped in front of him. Ex-Detective-Inspector Jackson had edged his way quietly and unassumingly to the side of Captain Egerton as they had all trooped in from the dining room, and was now seated next to him. The rest of the party had spread themselves out until they formed a half-moon round the fireplace.

'Er — before I begin,' said Mr. Whipple, 'there are two people who have not yet arrived, but whose presence is very necessary. I am referring to Inspector Gallers and Inspector Pepper. They were to have been here at nine o'clock, but something seems to have — er — delayed them. It is — er — essential, however, that we should wait, so I must ask you all to be as patient as possible for a little while longer.'

It was a very little while, for at that moment Hollick appeared to announce that Gallers and Pepper were in the hall.

'Ask them to come in,' said Shand. They came, Gallers apologizing for being late.

'The car skidded,' he explained, 'and it took us some time to get the back wheel out of a ditch, otherwise we should have been here on time.' He smiled a greeting to Mr. Whipple, while Dick found two chairs.

Inspector Pepper had assumed a rather exaggerated expression of boredom that was destined to disappear completely before Mr. Whipple had got very far with what he had to say. He gave them time to settle down and then he began.

'The killing of James Mortimer,' he said, speaking slowly and rather nervously, 'is unique in two ways. Firstly, because it represents that Mecca of the sensational novelist the almost perfect crime, and secondly because the murderer made no mistakes.

The — er — clue which enabled me eventually to discover the truth was something that was completely outside his control and — er — which he could not have guarded against. In order that what I'm going to say will be clearly understood by everybody I should like, briefly, to recapitulate the circumstances of the murder.'

He cleared his throat and went on:

'At nine-thirty-one this morning Detective-Inspector Gallers, while on his way to keep an appointment with James Mortimer, heard a shot from inside the latter's bedroom; and opening the door, which was unlocked, he discovered Mortimer lying across the sill of the open window, shot through the head. He gave the alarm, and I was the first to — er — reach him. I was just leaving the dining room, in which were Colonel Shand, his son, Inspector Jackson, Captain Egerton, John Ramsden and Miss Claire Weston. When I reached the corridor I found Inspector Gallers standing by the open door of Mortimer's room and he showed me what had happened.

'At first, since it was utterly impossible for anyone to have left the room between the time of that shot and Gallers' discovery of the body, we came to the conclusion that Mortimer had committed suicide; but when we discovered there were no powder marks round the wound — and no trace of any weapon this opinion had to be altered, and there was nothing left but — er — murder!'

He paused for a moment, moistened his lips.

'We made an examination of the room and discovered a partly finished letter which the dead man had evidently started and then discarded,' he continued. 'It referred to somebody who had apparently been persecuting him. In his hand, the right hand, we discovered a piece of coal tightly clasped; and on examining the wound where the bullet had made its exit we found that although it had bled, the coldness of the morning had frozen what blood there was and so had stopped it bleeding any further. Apart from the fact that everybody in the house, with the exception of Inspector Gallers, was provided with an alibi, they could, none of them, have fired that shot heard by Gallers at nine-thirty-one, because nobody could possibly have left the room after it was fired. Yet somebody had shot James Mortimer. That was the impossible problem, which, this morning, I — er — attempted to solve.'

He paused again for a moment. The silence in the room was intense, unbroken, except for the soft, quick breathing of his listeners.

'Then the police arrived,' he went on. 'Inspector Pepper's suspicions immediately centred on Gallers. In — er — justice to the inspector I must — er — say that had I not known — er — Inspector Gallers as well as I do I think mine would have done the same. But, knowing him, I was certain that however black appearances were against him, he had had no hand in the murder. But unless one was willing to accept Inspector Pepper's solution, the whole thing was an utter impossibility.

'Now, nothing that *has* happened can be impossible, and so I knew that there was an explanation. At first I must confess I could see no possible solution. I was blinded, like everybody else, by one glaring fact. This, of course, was the murderer's intention. He gave us the fact and expected us to take it for granted. I'm afraid I took it for granted, until, thinking the matter over, I remembered a rather curious circumstance. It was this: Shortly after the discovery of the body I looked out of the window. It had, as you all know, been snowing heavily throughout the night. The ground was covered with a thick carpet of snow, and this extended right up to the wall of the house, below the window of the room in which Mortimer had been killed.

'Now the dead man's body, when we found it, was lying across the sill with the head and shoulders protruding outside, and when I looked at the snow beneath it was white and unmarked. Since — er — apparently the freezing temperature had stopped the blood flowing from the wound this did not strike me as at all out of the way. But later, when Inspector

Gallers and I went downstairs to look for traces below the window of Mortimer's room, I found, to my utter astonishment, quite a different state of affairs. The snow was now deeply stained with blood, and so far as I could see at the time there was no accounting for this fact. It was only while I was trying to hit upon a solution to the mystery that the significance of this fact became plain to me. I saw exactly why the snow had been white when I first looked out of the window and later turned red. *It was because the wound had bled and stained the snow, afterwards freezing, which stopped the bleeding, This stain had also frozen and been covered up by a fresh layer of snow as it fell.*

'This was a simple explanation, but what it led to was not so simple. For I remembered, and I was prepared to swear, that the snow *had ceased falling at the time that Inspector Gallers and I discovered the crime.*'

He stopped, and his eyes, blinking rapidly, travelled swiftly from face to face. Only on one did he see that the full meaning of his words had been appreciated. John Ramsden was sitting forward, a look of incredulous amazement on his face, staring at him.

'Perhaps you will — er — understand better what this discovery meant,' Mr. Whipple went on, 'when I tell you that Hollick is willing to state on oath that *the snow stopped falling at nine-twenty-eight!*'

There came a gasp from Colonel Shand.

'Good God, Whipple,' he cried hoarsely, 'you don't mean — '

'I mean,' explained Mr. Whipple, 'that Gallers did not hear the shot fired until nine-thirty-one. The snow *had stopped falling three minutes before Mortimer was killed*, and therefore there was *no snow to cover up the stain below the window.*'

He waited, but nobody spoke.

'This led,' he continued, 'to only two conclusions. One that the blood had *not* come from the wound in Mortimer's head at all, but for some unknown reason and in some inexplicable way had been poured on to the snow after I had looked out of the window; or, two, that *Mortimer had been killed before the snow stopped falling.*'

'But,' exclaimed Gallers, 'that's impossible. I heard the sound of the shot!'

'You heard the sound of *a report,*' said Mr. Whipple swiftly, 'and when, immediately on top of it, you discovered a dead man with a bullet hole in his forehead in the room from which the sound of the report had come, you jumped to the conclusion that what you heard was the sound of the shot that killed him.'

'Are you suggesting, Whipple,' said the Chief Constable, 'that the shot we all heard was not the shot that killed Mortimer?'

Mr. Whipple nodded.

'Yes,' he answered. 'I am suggesting that Mortimer had been dead for *over half an hour* before the sound of that report led Gallers to discover his body.'

Inspector Pepper sprang to his feet.

'But it's ridiculous!' he protested. 'Somebody must have fired the shot that

Gallers heard, and there was nobody in the room!'

Mr. Whipple looked at him reproachfully.

'If you will have a little patience, Inspector,' he said, 'I will endeavour to — er — explain exactly how the murder was committed. I suggest that Mortimer had been dead over half an hour before the supposed time of his murder because of the amount of snow that would have had to fall in order to cover the bloodstain. Before we go any further I should like to point out that it was — er — still freezing hard at nine-thirty, and this would have accounted for the blood not oozing through its covering of snow until it began to thaw, which it did at approximately at nine-forty-five.

'When I had reached these — er — conclusions the whole case had, as you will see, taken on an entirely different aspect. The general alibi for everybody in the house *no longer held*. Although we knew where everyone was at *nine-thirty-one* we had no knowledge where they were at *eight-fifty*. The result of this was to give me a much wider scope in which to look for the murderer.'

There was an uneasy rustling among the semicircle of people as they shifted in their chairs, but if Mr. Whipple noticed it he made no sign, and went on in his slow, diffident manner:

'I am now going to tell you the 'how' of the crime,' he continued. 'And I should like to preface my statement by saying that this is not a theory but actual fact. I have evidence to prove it. I may as well begin by saying that the murderer had made up his mind to kill Mortimer before either he or the dead man entered this house. Not only had he made up his mind but he had practically formulated the plan by which the crime was to be carried out. Mortimer, as you will presently learn, was an assumed name. The dead man's real name was James Flagg, and he had suffered a term of imprisonment for embezzlement. The murderer had, for some years, been — er — blackmailing him because of this, gradually increasing his demands as he found how easy it was to — er — fleece his victim.

'Towards the end, however, he found that Mortimer was chafing under his persecution. Probably, he learned that in a case of blackmail the police are always willing to keep the identity of the blackmailed person a secret. Whether this was the case or not I cannot say, of course, and it's not of great importance. What Mortimer did do, however, was to threaten his persecutor with exposure, and by doing so he signed his — er — death warrant. The murderer realized that the goose had ceased laying the golden eggs, and for his own safety must be destroyed.

'The method he adopted was exceedingly clever. But for the snow, over which he had no control, I think he would have been successful in getting away with the crime without any suspicion falling on himself.

'I told you that shortly after the discovery of the body, Inspector Gallers and I found in the dead man's hand a piece of coal. The fire in the bedroom being a gas fire and there being no coal handy, it was a most unusual object to find, and for a long time I puzzled as to how it could have got there. The explanation, however, was very simple. The murderer, having decided to kill Mortimer and hit upon the idea by which he could put the crime forward half an hour and so provide himself with an alibi, found — er — purely by accident, owing to the arrangement of the rooms, that the actual shooting was going to be easier than he had expected. His first idea — this is conjecture on my part — had been to go into Mortimer's room, shoot him with a silenced pistol, arrange the mechanics for his alibi, and then come on down to breakfast so that when the sound of the report was heard he would have several people to swear that he was nowhere near the murdered man's room at the time.

'However, owing, as I say, to the allotment of the rooms, a much easier plan suggested itself, and this he adopted. Before going up to bed he provided himself with this — er — this piece of coal.'

Mr. Whipple took the lump from his

pocket and held it up between his fingers.

'When the time was ripe for the murder to be committed — and this was shortly before nine, I think — he tied some cotton to the coal, and leaning out of the window let the coal down on the end of the cotton until it hung opposite the window of Mortimer's bedroom. By swinging it gently he was able to make it rattle against the glass. Mortimer, hearing the taps and naturally wondering what caused them, opened his window and looked out. The murderer called to him softly, which made him turn his head upwards, and as he did so the man above shot him through the forehead. In collapsing across the sill, Mortimer grabbed at the lump of coal. The murderer jerked at the cotton, which became unfastened, leaving the coal in the dead man's hand. The murderer then hastily hid the pistol with its silencer, hurried downstairs to Mortimer's room, slipped in and placed under the gas-fire an ordinary cracker, such as one can obtain from any shop that sells fireworks, but attached to which was a fuse timed to last half an hour. This he lighted, left the room, and came downstairs to breakfast. The smell of cordite which we noticed in the corridor, and the report heard by Inspector Gallers, were due to the explosion of this cracker.'

Mr. Whipple stopped, a little breathless, and then, suddenly leaning forward he said, almost conversationally:

'That is correct, isn't it? That's how you did it, Jackson?'

10

THE KILLER

Jackson sprang from his chair, his face livid and convulsed with rage. His hand flew to his pocket and the light glinted bluely on the muzzle of the automatic. Before he could raise the weapon, however, Shand gripped his wrist and twisted it from his grasp. Jackson struck out. The blow caught the Chief Constable on the chin and sent him staggering backwards. Mrs. Ramsden screamed as he made a bound for the door, shouldering Colonel Shand out of the way as he tried to stop him.

By this time Inspector Pepper and Gallers had recovered from their first momentary shock of surprise; and they closed in on Jackson, one on either side, and as he struggled furiously Gallers shot out a foot and tripped him up. He fell heavily to the floor, dragging Pepper with him, and with a supreme effort succeeded in breaking away from the inspector's grip.

Before he could scramble to his feet, however, Gallers gripped him by the collar and grabbing his wrist with the other hand twisted his arm up behind his back.

'Wriggle out of that!' he grunted.

The ex-inspector, unable to move without breaking his arm, glared round at Mr. Whipple.

'You devil!' he muttered. 'I never thought you had the brains! If I'd only had a chance with that pistol — '

'I'm afraid it wouldn't have done you much good if you had,' said Mr. Whipple. 'I — er — took the precaution of loading it with blanks before giving it to you. You should have used the one you shot at us with in the drive!'

'I thought you suspected Egerton,' snarled Jackson.

'Dear me, did you?' Mr. Whipple resumed. 'I was afraid you would. In fact I — I rather wanted you to.'

'How did you find it all out?' muttered Jackson.

'Entirely through the snow,' answered the little man. 'That was the — er — the clue that put me on the right track. The rest was merely imagination. When I had evolved this imaginary theory that fitted all the facts I proceeded to test it to see if it was the right one. I found a small portion of the exploded cracker under the gas-fire in Mortimer's bedroom. The first thing that suggested to me the use to which the coal had been put was the mark on the windowpane where it had struck. When I discovered the bullet flattened out against a stone on the ground below, it was really very easy.'

'But how did you know it was me?' said Jackson.

Mr. Whipple shrugged his shoulders.

'Really, I shouldn't have thought you need ask that,' he replied. 'As soon as I knew the murder had been committed earlier than it appeared, I guessed you were the murderer. That half-finished letter with the words 'your superiors' made me suspect you, although at the time I couldn't see how you — er — could have done it. It was obvious Mortimer was referring to somebody who was, or had been, connected with the police. 'Your superiors will deal with you' or 'your superiors will take action' — he had been going to say something like that, but I'll admit it was only suspicion then. I didn't know for a certainty until after I had phoned up Scotland Yard and learned from them that it was you who had arrested Mortimer, or Flagg, for the embezzlement fifteen years ago. When I knew that, and when Colonel Shand very kindly gave me a list of the various occupants of the rooms and I found that your room was the one immediately above Mortimer's, I was certain whom I had to deal with.'

'If I'd only known,' muttered Jackson. 'If I'd only thought you could have found it out.'

'You'd have tried something before you tried to kill me in the drive?' said Mr. Whipple. 'Yes, I expect you would, but you weren't afraid that anyone would suspect you until you heard that I was going to Mortimer's house. You weren't sure then what Mortimer might have left behind. You'd already taken his latch-key, hadn't you, with the intention of going over yourself and destroying any incriminating evidence there might be?'

Jackson nodded dully; his demeanour had suddenly changed. The rage had died out of his face, leaving it calm and rather tired.

'Yes, I was going,' he said. 'And then I was afraid to leave; I thought it might look suspicious. Well, I played for big stakes and I've lost. A police pension isn't a lot of money to retire on, and when I came to live here for the sake of cheapness and saw Mortimer and recognized him as Flagg, I thought I might augment the pittance that I had got. Most of the money I got from him I've invested, and if I had succeeded in getting away with this killing the income from that and my pension would have kept me in comfort for the rest of my life.' He stopped, and passed his tongue over his dry lips. 'Well, I lost,' he said, 'and you won, but I'd like to say one thing. I had no intention of throwing the blame on Gallers. That was an accident. I suppose Mortimer decided to tell him all about it?'

'I think he was writing that letter to send to Scotland Yard,' said Mr. Whipple, 'when he remembered there was an official from Scotland Yard in the same house.' He blinked at the ex-detective. 'As a matter of curiosity,' he said, 'I wish you'd tell me one thing. How did you get out to fire those shots in the drive and get back again without being seen by anyone in the house?'

'Through the library window,' answered Jackson. 'I was alone in the library, pretending to do a crossword puzzle, and wondering what you might have discovered. I was afraid of you from the start because I'd heard about that business at East Gables. I slipped out of the window and round to the drive. When I saw that my attempt had failed I re-entered the house in the same way, wiped the mud off my shoes with my handkerchief and came out into the hall as though I'd been doing a crossword puzzle all the time.'

Inspector Pepper, who had regained his feet and his official pompousness, cleared his throat portentously.

'Henry Jackson,' he said gruffly, 'I arrest you for the murder of James Flagg, alias James Mortimer, and I must warn you that anything you say will . . . '

GRIM DEATH
MURDER IN MANUSCRIPT
THE GLASS ARROW
THE THIRD KEY
THE ROYAL FLUSH MURDERS
THE SQUEALER